WORTH FIGHTING FOR

Book One of the Worth It Series

ANGIE BATHO-BARTH

ISBN-13: 978-1519445285

ISBN-10: 1519445288

Cover Picture:
http://www.fanpop.com/clubs/trees/images/31754189/title/tree-lined-path-photo

Author Photo:
By Cassie Martin Photography
http://www.cassiemartinphotography.com/

Acknowledgments

It may sound cliché, but this book would not exist without God. He would flood my mind with ideas to the point that my head hurt and showed me how to weave together people and events from my own life with fictitious elements to form a story I could never have created on my own.

It was through my involvement with Community Bible Study that I found the Scripture used within this novel. I love when God shows us how His Word, written thousands of years ago, still applies so powerfully and perfectly to our lives today.

It was also through CBS that I met Susanne. The story of precious Darlene Grace is her story. I remember the tears, the strength and the faith she shared when she told us her story. I am in awe of her and how she continues to use her story for God's glory.

To my dear family and friends: Thank you for your words of encouragement and support as I tried to keep my head above the sea of doubt I found myself in more days than not (James 1:6-8). Your words and Philippians 4:6 gave me the courage to take this leap of faith. May God speak to you through this story as He did me. Happy Reading and God Bless!

For
Darlene Grace

CHAPTER ONE

Mollie enjoyed the quiet after a long day of teaching. Brett wouldn't be home for a couple of hours, which gave her plenty of time to run errands or tidy up the apartment; anything that could get in the way of their time together. And even though this allowed for more quality time together, she couldn't shake the feeling that it was never enough. Brett has felt it too. He shocked everyone, especially Mollie, when he proposed on the Fourth of July; only a month after they met. He told her that he felt God pressing it upon his heart not to wait. And now, as she looked at the pictures on the wall, it didn't seem possible that a year and a half had passed and they were about to celebrate their six month wedding anniversary.

They agreed that there would be no gifts, but Mollie desperately wanted to get Brett something. Yet, no matter what she came up with, nothing compared to the first gift she gave him. It was a necklace with a cross made out of three nails and a dog tag with Jeremiah 29:11 etched on it: "'I know the plans that I have for you,' declares the Lord, 'plans for prosperity and not for calamity, to give you a future and a hope.[1]'"

God had definitely done just that. For the past year and a half there had been no talk of another deployment. Mollie knew that marrying a Marine came with the possibility of him having to fight overseas, but, after what he went through the last time, she prayed daily that God would spare him from another tour.

The thought sent chills up her spine as her mind drifted back to the moment when Brett confided in her about his experience in Afghanistan. While he was there he was constantly looking over his shoulder because the enemy had gone underground, disguising themselves as civilians. No one could be trusted. It was no wonder he suffered from flashbacks the moment he returned home.

It didn't seem fair that after fighting for his country that Brett would then suffer because of it. Yet, through it all, Brett still tells Mollie how thankful he is for having had those flashbacks. He believes that without them, they might not have ended up together. Mollie was sure they would have met eventually, especially considering Brett's sister, Brooke, is Mollie's best friend. But it never seemed to work out for them to meet; not until after his tour in Afghanistan.

After returning to the states, Brett went to stay with his parents, but the flashbacks were taking a toll on him, and them. He hated seeing the pain and helplessness in his parents' eyes. So, he asked his sister Brooke if he could come for a visit. Brooke and Mollie had been roommates ever since their freshman year of college. In all that time Mollie had met all of Brooke's family *except* Brett. But that didn't stop her from being just as eager as Brooke to help him.

That first night of Brett's visit was full of memorable moments. Just the thought of it still brings warmth to Mollie's cheeks. There she was in the kitchen, singing and dancing as she put dishes away, completely oblivious to the fact that Brooke and Brett had walked in and were watching her. That was the first time she saw his intoxicating smile. That in itself made up for her complete and utter embarrassment.

Later that same night she had prayed that God would use her to help Brett. Little did she know that God's plan was to have her pray over Brett. She was comfortable with praying *for* someone, but definitely not praying *over* someone, especially someone she had just met and was instantly attracted to. Only by the grace of God did she have the courage to do what He asked. To this day, Brooke believes that Mollie's prayers over Brett are the reason his flashbacks went away. Ultimately, they know it was all God. Not only did the experience deepen Brett's relationship with God, but also with Mollie.

Mollie gently touched the base of her neck. It was habit; a habit she was trying desperately to break. Instead, every time she was reminded of the necklace Brett had given her shortly after being engaged; the necklace she lost. Mollie wore it every day and was devastated when she realized it was gone. She had retraced her steps in a desperate effort to find it but to no avail. She could still picture it...a delicate silver chain with a tiny heart and a small cross hanging from it.

Brett said that when he saw the necklace it instantly reminded him of her because he could tell from the moment they met that she had Jesus in her heart. Mollie searched website after website trying to find a replacement, but it was nowhere to be found. She would give anything to have her necklace back. As she looked up she noticed the clock on the wall. *Brett will be home soon. That is, if he isn't running late...again...*

Brett was still at the office trying to get through the remaining stack of papers on his desk. As much as he tried to focus on his work, he couldn't keep from looking up at the clock. Maybe it was because he knew that Mollie was already home waiting for him. Ever since the day they met he has felt this urgent need to be with her. At first, he thought that it was merely infatuation. But after *a lot* of careful thought and prayer, Brett realized that his feelings for her were genuine and that God was nudging him to do something that didn't make sense to a lot of people, his sister included.

Even though Brett's sister, Brooke, has been Mollie's best friend and roommate since college and loves her like a sister, she was still shocked when he told her that he planned to ask Mollie to marry him, especially since he had only known Mollie for a little over a month. And Brett didn't intend to steal any of the spotlight from Brooke and her fiance Derek, but he couldn't fight the feeling that he needed to act now. Brett also hadn't planned on people making negative assumptions as to why they had gotten engaged so quickly. But here they were, six months into their marriage, proving to the world that their love is real and centered around God.

After tidying things up at his desk, Brett made his way to his car. As he pulled onto the interstate, a bright blue Camaro sped by. Brett had once dreamed of owning a car like that. He and Mollie even joked about getting a BMW since it matched their initials: Brett and Mollie Walker. But they both knew that saving up for a home and a future family was more important than some fancy car. Suddenly, his thoughts were interrupted by the sound of his phone ringing. His heart instantly started racing. Brett hated keeping secrets from Mollie. She would know soon enough, and he prayed that she would understand. He hoped that making this extra stop on the way home would not take too long. He didn't want Mollie to get suspicious...

Blake Williams *loved* his new, blue Camaro. The way he could maneuver effortlessly around cars, especially on the interstate, was exhilarating. *Yes siree Blake Williams, you have arrived!* Blake loved hearing those words echo in his mind. Life seemed to have fallen into place four months ago when he *finally* got a promotion. The timing couldn't have been more perfect. His roommate was about to move out and, if Blake hadn't gotten this promotion, he would have needed to move too. But with this new position came a big bump in pay, so Blake could easily swing the rent on his own. He would be locked into a lease for another year but that was okay. He didn't plan on going anywhere.

Renting an apartment on his own wasn't Blake's only splurge. He had just bought this brand new, bright blue Chevy Camaro. It wasn't practical but, hey, he was still young. Practical ...now that's a word Blake's mother loved to use. She was sure to use it when he told her about the new job.

"Oh honey! That's wonderful! What an answer to prayer."

She always had a way of throwing God into the conversation. Blake loved his parents dearly but he just didn't have the same type of faith that they did. He didn't see the point in bothering God, or bothering *with* Him. *Blake* studied hard in college. *He* worked hard at his career. *He* got this promotion. The way Blake saw it, *he* was doing pretty well on his own.

When he told his mom about his plans with the apartment and wanting to buy a new car the joy in her voice instantly turned to concern. "Blake, are you sure you should be taking on so much? The economy is still a bit shaky. The practical thing to do would be to find another roommate and hold off a little while on the new car."

There she goes again. This wouldn't be the first time Blake made a decision that his mother did not agree with, and he knew it wouldn't be the last. Besides, she had nothing to be worried about. Blake *would* have a roommate soon enough. His girlfriend, Abby, planned to move in with him once her lease ran out. But Blake couldn't tell his mom just yet. She wouldn't think it was *practical*.

CHAPTER TWO

Normally, Blake couldn't wait for Friday to roll around, but after the past few days, he was almost sad to see the week come to an end. Not once, but on three separate occasions, Blake's boss had called him into his office to tell him what a great job he was doing. Even though this promotion was a major step forward, Blake was already setting his sights for something bigger, something better. He was going to do whatever it took to do his job well and impress the right people.

So, when Blake's boss called him into his office shortly before it was time to leave for the day, Blake thought he needed to pinch himself. *Really? Four times in one week?* But, as soon as Blake walked into his boss' office, he knew something was different.

"Hi Blake. Have a seat," he said, barely able to make eye contact.

"Blake, as you know, we have done some expanding lately, adding departments and staff, in hopes that the economy would turn around. Well, that just hasn't happened yet and the powers that be want us to make cuts, major cuts. We are going to have to consolidate departments and your department is one of them. It will be merged with Marty's. With all this consolidating we won't need as many managers as we currently have. I'm sorry Blake. You have been doing an exceptional job, but Marty has more experience, more seniority. We are letting you go. Today will be your last day."

"What? I...I don't understand! They couldn't have given me a warning that this was coming? No two week notice?" Blake asked, his heart beating wildly.

"Because of the nature of your job and the information you are privy to, we couldn't let you know until today. Blake, I am so sorry," he replied, looking down.

"Can I at least get my old job back?" Blake asked, anxiety seizing every inch of him.

"Blake, they are making some drastic cuts. I'm so sorry. There isn't anything we can offer you at this time."

Blake felt as if the walls were closing in on him. He needed to get out of there. Somehow, Blake managed to get to his car. He couldn't seem to catch his breath and his heart felt like it was on the verge of exploding. After taking some deep breaths, he started the car. He knew that Abby wasn't expecting him for another hour or so but he had to see her. He needed her.

Blake knocked on Abby's door. No answer. He'd seen her car in the parking lot. *Where is she?* He knocked again. Again, no answer. He reached into his pocket and retrieved the key to Abby's apartment that she had given him weeks ago. He unlocked the door and stepped inside. That's when Blake saw him; a half-naked man racing across the living room grabbing for a pair of shoes. Blake searched the room, looking for Abby. *She has a roommate so maybe this is her boyfriend.* Suddenly, Abby appeared from her bedroom. Her hair was disheveled and her shirt was on backwards.

"What? Abby! What's going on?" Blake demanded.

"Blake! I'm so sorry! I was going to tell you! I never meant for you to find out like this. It...it just happened," she sobbed.

"You're...you're *cheating* on me?" he asked, anger boiling up inside him.

"I didn't mean for this to happen. It just...did. I was going to tell you tonight. Blake, I'm so sorry," she said as she fell to her knees.

"Tell me *what?*" Blake asked through clenched teeth.

"That I have fallen in love with someone else," she wailed, holding her head in her hands.

Blake wanted to hit...something. Instead he spun around, walked out and slammed the door behind him.

Blake's mind was racing as he got into his car. So much had happened in the past hour, and his brain was desperately trying to put it all together. He just caught the woman he loves and planned to marry with another man. With no job and little to no prospects for another, Blake was sure he would be homeless soon and it would only be a matter of time before the bank would come after his car. He had officially lost everything.

Blake thought about calling his mom. The thought made him clench his jaw and throw his phone onto the passenger side floor. Even though his mother would be gentle with her words he *knew* what she would be thinking. *Why didn't he listen? Why wasn't he more practical?* The last thing Blake needed was to feel judged. She would tell him to pray. *Right, so I can have God judging me too? No thanks.* Blake knew exactly what to do to make all this go away.

CHAPTER THREE

It was finally Friday night and Mollie was quickly tidying up the apartment before getting ready for their date. A thought kept haunting her as she scurried from room to room; Brett seemed different this week. Not only was he still coming home later than usual, but he also seemed distant, like there was something on his mind. *Maybe it is something with work. Hopefully a romantic dinner and a weekend alone together will turn things around...*

W

Brett couldn't get home soon enough. He had so much to tell Mollie, to show her. He thought about doing it at the restaurant but didn't want to make a scene. He could tell that she sensed that something was up. Tonight was the night; he couldn't keep these things from her any longer.

Mollie greeted Brett at the door. When he saw her he couldn't help himself; he had to hold her, to kiss her. Brett quickly changed clothes and they were on their way to the restaurant. He was thankful that they were seated at an intimate table for two near a window.

"I don't know if it is possible, but you look more beautiful today than the day I met you," he said as he took Mollie's hands in his and gazed into her blue eyes.

"Well, that sounds possible to me, considering I was dancing and singing around the kitchen when we first met," she chuckled.

"You made me smile. I hadn't been able to do that in quite a while," he replied, gently caressing her hands.

"After all you had been through it is no wonder you had trouble smiling. I thank God every day that your flashbacks have not returned."

"Me too," Brett added, kissing her hand. "I believe that God was working through you when you prayed over me. The fact that you did that, something completely out of your comfort zone, spoke volumes about the type of person you are. And then, as if what you did wasn't enough, you bought me a gift! Who would have known that the necklace you gave me would open so many doors for me to share my faith and be a witness for God?"

"Well, that's easy. God knew," Mollie chuckled again.

"Beauty *and* brains. I got the total package when I married you," he laughed.

"Me too," she added.

"To think, I almost missed my chance. It took you a while to tell me about the other guy," he said with a little grin.

"Who? Oh, you mean Mitch! You say that as if it had been serious."

"Well, serious enough to date," Brett replied, his grin growing wider.

"You *know* we only went out a few times. I taught with his mom and she introduced us the day after you left. At first I thought it was God's way of telling me to move on and forget my feelings for you. But when Mitch shared with me that he did not believe in God I knew we couldn't be more than friends. I told God that I would rather be single than settle, especially when it came to faith. Besides," she said, leaning toward Brett, "I was comparing him to you the whole time. And you know what my mom had to say about you?" Mollie asked, leaning even closer.

"No. What?" he asked, desperately wanting to kiss her.

"She said that the reason I kept comparing Mitch to you is because you possess the qualities that I admire and look for in a person."

"Wow! That ranks up there with her telling you that she had been praying for your future husband and that God was showing off when He placed me in your life."

"My mom is a pretty wise person," Mollie whispered and gave him a long, soft kiss. Instantly, Brett's whole body felt like it was on fire. He couldn't wait to get home.

"Remember how pouty I was when the rain stopped us from having an outdoor wedding?" she asked, drawing Brett back from his thoughts of desire.

"I love when you pout. You look adorable with that beautiful bottom lip sticking out."

"But then God showed up and showed off with that incredible rainbow just as we were leaving the church," she said, a light in her eyes.

"It *was* incredible. And so was the fireworks display you surprised me with after the reception. It brought everything full-circle," Brett added.

"There were so many wonderful moments and surprises throughout the entire day. Like when you asked to see me before the wedding. I was worried that something was wrong, and I still didn't want us to see each other before the ceremony."

"I wanted a moment alone to pray together. I'm so sorry if I made you worry," Brett said apologetically.

Mollie ran her fingers along Brett's face. "You were honoring God through our prayer and honoring me by standing on one side of the door while I was on the other. I thought I was ready for anything after our prayer, but I was wrong. When I entered the sanctuary and saw you standing there in *full* uniform, I thought my knees would give out," she chuckled.

"What about you? I knew you would be beautiful, but I was not prepared for how absolutely stunning you were. You took my breath away," he said as he moved his chair closer to hers.

"I'm glad we waited to see each other until the ceremony started," she added.

"That's not the only thing I'm glad we waited for," Brett whispered, his chair right next to hers.

Her face instantly turned red. Oh, how Brett loved seeing her blush.

"There were so many times I didn't think I could hold on while we held off until our wedding night," he whispered, his mouth close to her cheek.

"Only by the grace of God," she whispered as she turned her face toward Brett.

He kissed her long and hard. It *had* been by the grace of God. After experiencing the passion of their first kiss when Brett proposed, they realized that they needed to set some boundaries. They never allowed themselves to be alone together and they limited physical contact to holding hands. Even with all these precautions in place there were times when Brett wasn't sure he could restrain himself. There were also times when others would make jokes about their courting. But they knew they were honoring God, and each other, by waiting. And their wedding night was proof that God's ways are far better than the ways of the world.

"Thankfully we don't have to wait anymore. How about we get out of here? I have a surprise for you," he whispered softly in her ear.

Mollie was instantly covered in goose bumps and her body felt as if electricity were pulsating through it. They quickly grabbed their things and headed for the car.

"You didn't get me a gift did you? We said no gifts," Mollie said as they got into the car.

Brett turned toward her and flashed that handsome grin that won her over the day they met.

"I guess you'll just have to wait and see, won't you?" he said, taking her hand in his. There was such a gentleness, a genuineness, in the way Brett expressed his love for Mollie. Her mom was right; God had outdone Himself when He made Brett.

As Brett drove, Mollie heard her phone beep. It was a text from Brooke wishing them a happy anniversary. Mollie was in the middle of texting Brooke back when she heard Brett scream out, "NO!"

Mollie quickly looked up to see what was wrong, but all she could see was a brilliant white light.

CHAPTER FOUR

Mollie desperately tried to open her eyes. They budged a little, enough for her to see that brilliant white light again. She could hear voices and there was something hovering over her. She tried blinking, hoping to see better. Each time Mollie blinked the image became clearer. It was her mom. *Why are her eyes red? Has she been crying? What did she just say? Thank you sweet Jesus? What is going on?*

Mollie felt a hand on her shoulder. "Just relax honey. It's going to be okay." It was her dad. She slowly turned her head in the direction of his voice. The pain was excruciating. Every inch of her body ached. *What is happening? Where am I?* Slowly, more of her senses came alive. She could hear machines whirring and beeping. The bright lights were fluorescent bulbs hanging above her. Mollie tried to look around the room. She could see Brooke and Derek in the corner. Brooke was sobbing.

Mollie tried to speak but only a moan emerged from her lips. *What is wrong with me?* She tried again, focusing on forming the words. "Wh...Wh...What?" Her parents knew what she was trying to say. They looked at each other as if they were trying to figure out what they should tell her. Mollie was getting impatient. She wanted to know what was going on and she wanted to know *now*!

"Mollie, you were in a car accident. Someone crossed over into your lane and hit you. You are pretty beat up but the doctors say you should make a full recovery," her dad said, his voice trembling.

So why is Brooke crying? The doctors say I am going to be fine. How is the other dri-? Mollie's brain had finally caught up and she began to remember what had happened before the accident. She

14

was with *Brett!* *Where's Brett?* *Is he okay?* Mollie tried desperately to say the words but all that came out was, "Brett?"

Her mother started weeping. Mollie's dad steadied himself and gently touched her face, "Mollie, Brett is with Jesus."

"No!" she moaned. Deep sobs overcame her and inflicted pain throughout her entire being. She wanted to die. *Why, Lord? Why didn't you take me too? I can't live without him! The doctors are wrong. I will never fully recover from this!*

Mollie spent the next few days crying and sleeping. A nurse would come in now and then to give her something to help with the pain but there was no drug that was going to take away the pain she was experiencing. Brett was gone. The only shred of peace Mollie found was knowing that he was in Heaven and that, one day, she would be with him again. When she wasn't crying, she was praying that God would change His mind and take her too.

Mollie's mom never left her side. She held Mollie's hand just like Brett did right before the... Mollie wanted answers. *How could this have happened?* Her mom said that the police were still investigating the accident and should have a final report soon. *Soon? When will that be?*

Mollie couldn't stand staying in the hospital any longer than necessary. She wanted to get home, to *their* home. She mentally prepared herself for the pain she would endure during the car ride and the walk to the apartment. Her body had definitely taken a beating in the accident and it was still painful to do even the simplest of tasks. The doctor prescribed some pain killers to help her get through the next few weeks.

Mollie's mom, Karen, offered to stay with her. After they left the hospital, they stopped at the pharmacy to pick up the prescription. Mollie took one of the pills right away as they drove to her apartment complex. By the time they pulled into the parking lot, Mollie could tell that the medicine was beginning to work. But, as soon as Mollie walked through the door of their home, she was consumed with a pain that even the strongest medicine in the world couldn't fix. All around their apartment were pictures;

wedding pictures, snapshots. So many wonderful memories and now there would be no more memories, no more wonderful moments together. Mollie curled up on the couch and let the tears come.

Karen offered to go to the grocery store and get a few things. Mollie was thankful for her help and how she knew when Mollie needed a little time to herself. Shortly after Karen left, Mollie managed to get up off the couch and make her way to the bedroom. She went straight for their closet and found one of Brett's shirts in the hamper. Mollie nuzzled her face into the shirt taking in the familiar scent of his cologne. Slowly, she turned to go back to the living room. She couldn't bear to be in the bedroom any longer. Too many memories of the love they shared were overflowing in that room.

Out of the corner of her eye she saw a small gift bag on the floor of the closet, somewhat tucked away under Brett's dress pants. Mollie gently lifted the bag. *Is this the surprise? Did he get me a gift after all?* She walked, as quickly as her body would allow, back to the living room. She was almost to the couch when she heard someone knock on the door. *Could that be Mom? Back so soon? But, she has a key. Why would she knock?*

Mollie looked through the peephole and saw a police officer standing in the hall. She quickly opened the door.

"Hello ma'am. Are you Mrs. Walker? Mrs. Mollie Anne Walker?" the officer asked.

"Yes, yes I am," she managed to reply, clutching Brett's shirt. Hearing him call her Mrs. Walker nearly brought her to her knees.

"Ma'am, our department has concluded its investigation into your automobile accident, and I am here to deliver the final report," he said, handing her a manila envelope.

Mollie's hand shook as she took the envelope.

"I am so sorry for your loss, Mrs. Walker." There was a kindness in his eyes that let her know he was being genuine, not just doing his job.

"Thank you," she whispered before closing the door.

Back inside the apartment she slowly made her way to the couch. She placed the envelope and the gift bag on the coffee table. Mollie stared at each of them, wondering which one she should open first. She reached for the manilla envelope. She didn't want not knowing its contents to distract her when she opens the gift bag, especially if there was a gift inside of it from Brett.

Mollie began to gently open the envelope. Ever since the accident, she has had numerous scenarios play out in her mind as to what may have caused the accident. *Maybe the other driver had a seizure, a stroke, maybe a heart attack... something beyond his control.* The only information she had been given so far is that the other driver is male. Now she would finally have some concrete answers. Her eyes scanned the papers, looking for the place where they concluded what caused the accident.

There, at the bottom of the second page was her answer. When she read it her blood began to boil. *The other driver was...drunk! There was no medical emergency that caused him to wander into our lane. No, this was one hundred percent preventable. This person chose to drink and drive and Brett paid the price.* Mollie wanted this man to pay, and pay dearly for what he took from her.

Only after her jaw started to hurt did she notice just how tightly her teeth were clenched. She relaxed, but only a little. Mollie looked at the gift bag. She didn't want to be angry when she opened it, but at the same time, she was desperate for a connection to Brett. She had peered into the bag earlier and saw a small box and an envelope. Whatever was in that envelope may be some of the last words Brett wrote before the accident. Mollie took a few deep breaths. She needed to get under control so she could focus on Brett. *I will not let that drunk driver rob me of the joy of whatever might be inside that bag. He has already taken enough from me!*

Mollie reached into the bag and pulled out the envelope and the box. On the outside of the envelope it said, "Read me first." Tears quietly fell from her cheeks as she gently ran her fingers over the words. Those quiet tears became deep sobs as she read Brett's words. Mollie reached for the box. Inside the box was a note. The note brought her thoughts back to something else that was written in the police report. She began to wail. She clung to the contents of the box. *It's all my fault! I want to be with Brett! I want this pain to go away! I want to go Home!*

CHAPTER FIVE

By the time Karen got to the supermarket it was an absolute zoo. The trip was already taking longer than she had planned and now she was bobbing and weaving around cart after cart. But it *was* five thirty on a weekday. She assumed that most of the people there had just gotten done with work and were making a quick stop at the grocery store before resuming with the hustle and bustle of their lives. How Karen wished her daughter was one of them. Instead, this accident, this tragedy, had brought Mollie's life to a screeching halt. And Karen couldn't shake this uneasy feeling that even with all the love and support of her family and friends, and the foundation of her faith, Mollie would never fully recover from what had happened.

Suddenly, another feeling came over Karen, a sense of urgency. Her daughter needed her. Something was wrong, very wrong. She quickly paid for the items and sped back to the apartment. When Karen walked in all the lights were on and Mollie was lying on the couch. *What was I so worried about? She's just resting. She needs her rest.*

Karen quietly walked over to the kitchen to put the groceries away. She looked over at Mollie again and noticed that she was lying face down on the couch. Next to her, on the coffee table was a gift bag, some papers and...her prescription! *No! Dear God, No! She didn't!*

Karen rushed over to the couch and began frantically shaking Mollie. *Please, Lord! I never should have left her alone! Lord, please help me!*

"Mollie! Wake up! Please wake up!" Karen screamed, shaking her. *Please Lord, please let her wake up!*

Karen's heart leapt out of her chest when she saw her daughter's eyes flutter open. Mollie stared back at her with a look that broke Karen's heart. To see such pain and sorrow in her daughter's eyes was more than she could take. Mollie fell toward her and began to sob.

"Mollie? Mollie, what is it, what's wrong?" Karen asked, trying to understand why she was so upset. Mollie managed to reach for a piece of paper and handed it to Karen. Then she fell back onto the couch, clinging to Brett's shirt.

Karen scanned the page and realized it was a letter from Brett. Tears came quickly as she read his words.

Mollie-My gift from God,

I can't believe that we are celebrating our six month wedding anniversary! They say, "Time flies when you are having fun," and that definitely holds true when it comes to me and you. Married life has certainly been an adjustment for the both of us, but I could not imagine spending my life with anyone else. Not a day goes by that I don't thank God for placing you in my life. Because of you, my faith has been renewed and my heart is full of a joy and love I never knew existed.

God has blessed us immensely so far, and I wait with anticipation to see what He has in store for our future. And speaking of our future...there is something I need to tell you. Recently there have been talks of our unit being deployed. It wouldn't happen for several months, but I feel it's necessary to tell you right away so we can both prepare for it.

This latest news, this deployment, has really got me thinking. We both have said that every day is a gift and that only God knows when our time on Earth is done. I know we planned on waiting a couple of years, but... I was wondering if we could start trying to have a baby now instead of waiting.

I know it is a big decision and I want you to take all the time you need to be sure, especially since I could possibly be away during most of the pregnancy and potentially miss out on his/her first months. Something keeps telling me not to wait. Just like when I proposed to you, I keep feeling God nudging me.

And there's one more thing. I have been thinking and praying about this for the past few months. The necklace you gave me has opened the door for others to ask about my faith, and lately I have felt this calling, this pressing upon my heart, to become a pastor. So, with your support, I would like to start seminary school once this tour is done. I have never felt more alive than when I am with you and when I am telling others about Jesus.

So, what do you say? Want to make a baby? Want to be a pastor's wife? No matter what your decision, I love you, I always will until the day I die.

Love,
Brett

Brett really was all Karen had hoped for when she prayed all those years for Mollie's future husband. *How could God have taken him so soon?* Karen was thankful that her daughter wouldn't have to go through the constant worry of having her husband overseas. But having him tragically removed from her life was definitely *not* an easier alternative. *He wanted to be a pastor? Lord, why would You take him when he wanted to dedicate his life to reaching others in Your name?*

Mollie was still crying as Karen quietly reached for the small piece of paper on the coffee table. As she read, she felt herself begin to weep.

Mollie,
I know we said no gifts but I also know how upset you have been ever since the necklace I gave you disappeared. God placed an idea and a verse in my head and on my heart, so I hope you can forgive me for breaking our no-gift rule.

"There is no greater love than to lay down one's life for one's friends.[2]"

Jesus loves us so much that He laid down His life for us so that we may have eternal life with Him. Mollie, I would gladly lay down my own life for you. I love you with all that is in me and I will spend the rest of my life showing you my love.

P.S. I'm sorry for coming home late the past few weeks. I was working with a friend to have this made. It is a one-of-a-kind, just like you.

Love,
Brett

Karen's whole body was shaking as she reached for the box. Inside was a silver heart necklace. She picked up the necklace and studied it. The heart was made out of two hands. The thumbs created the top of the heart and the other fingers came together to form the point. The chain somehow went through the heart. As she looked closer, she discovered that the chain was going through two small holes, one on each of the palms of the hands. *These are Jesus' hands! These are the holes that were made when they nailed Him to the cross!*

For as long as Karen could remember, she has always been quick to say, "It is God's will," whenever there has been a blessing or tragedy. But now, after reading Brett's words of love and seeing the despair in her daughter's eyes, she struggled to understand how any of this could be used for God's good. *"Trust in the LORD with all your heart and lean not on your own understanding.[3]"*

Karen placed her hand on Mollie's shoulder. "Mollie?" she whispered, struggling to speak.

Mollie turned and threw herself on Karen. "Mom, it's my fault! It's all my fault!" she wailed.

Both Mollie's actions and her words caught Karen off-guard and they almost toppled onto the floor. Karen's mind started racing, trying to understand how Mollie could possibly think any of this was her fault. Karen gently stroked her daughter's hair, waiting for her sobbing to subside. Finally, Mollie pulled back and looked her in the eyes.

"Mom, every day since Brett and I got engaged I have been praying," she began sobbing again. Karen held her and gently rocked her, not knowing what to say. Mollie pulled back again and stammered, "I've been praying that Brett would not have another tour. I didn't think God would answer my prayer like...like *this*," she wailed and fell back into her mother's arms. Hot, fresh tears fell down Karen's cheeks. She didn't know how to respond. *Lord, I need Your Word to help me, to help her.* Suddenly, those same words came to her. *"Trust in the LORD with all your heart and lean not on your own understanding.*[3]*"*

Right now, nothing about this accident was making sense. How could Karen possibly tell her daughter that God can bring good from all of this when Mollie feels as though her whole world has come crashing down around her? Suddenly, God reminded Karen of a verse she had found while Mollie was in the hospital. *I need to find that verse! She needs to hear God's Word; that it will be okay!*

For now, all Karen could do was hold Mollie and let her know that she was not alone. Suddenly, Mollie pulled back hard, looking at her mother. "There's more," she exclaimed. She grabbed a stack of papers and feverishly looked over them. Mollie thrust a paper at her mother and pointed toward the bottom of the page. Karen began reading it and suddenly remembered the note and a new wave of tears emerged.

"It's all my fault!" Mollie screamed and fell onto the couch again. In the report, the officer concluded that Brett had steered hard right when he saw the oncoming car. His actions are what saved Mollie but it also meant that the majority of the impact was directed to the driver's side, killing Brett instantly. He *had* laid down his life for Mollie, just like the verse on the note! *Lord, how can I possibly help her? Please, show me!* And, in an instant, God answered Karen's prayer.

CHAPTER SIX

Mollie spent most of the next few days sleeping. Karen knew it was Mollie's coping mechanism; sleep quieted her thoughts and her emotions. They also discovered that Mollie's pain medication made her extremely tired, something Karen learned the hard way when she came home from the grocery store that first day and thought Mollie had…

So many emotions were running through Mollie: guilt, anger, depression, grief. Karen was thankful for the times when she was resting. It gave Karen time to work on the project that God had placed on her heart. And it gave her a break from seeing the excruciating pain in Mollie's eyes. Karen would give anything to be able to take that pain away.

Brett's visitation was only a few hours away and the funeral tomorrow. Brooke and the rest of Brett's family had taken care of all the preparations. Karen made sure to check in often with Brooke to see if there was anything they could do to help. Brooke reassured her that even though they were still in disbelief, they had come together as a family and gotten everything arranged. Mollie would make polite conversation anytime Brooke called or texted but Karen could tell that even the slightest human interaction was both physically and emotionally draining. She wondered how Mollie would make it through the next twenty-four hours.

Karen and Mollie arrived at the funeral home before any of the others so that Mollie could have some time alone with Brett. Her body still ached any time she moved, but it paled in comparison to the aching in her heart. She felt her heart race as she inched her way toward Brett. He looked so peaceful. She felt the familiar dampness on her cheeks. Over the past week, crying had become a lot like breathing, something that came without thinking; so much so that she rarely even noticed the tears anymore.

Seeing Brett in his uniform reminded Mollie of all the ways he demonstrated his love for her. He was always full of surprises that took her breath away and made her heart burst with a joy she had never felt before; a joy Mollie was sure she would never experience again.

Her mind drifted back to memories from the past year and a half… the first time she saw him in full uniform on their wedding day, their first kiss as husband and wife, Brett adorning their honeymoon suite with what seemed like a hundred candles and then sharing their first…everything. And now…now, he had given her a gift so precious, so special, and she wasn't able to show him how much it meant, how much *he* meant to her.

That's when Mollie saw it…Brett was wearing the necklace she had given him! She felt rage building up inside her. *You know the plans for me Lord? Plans to prosper and not for calamity? A future? A hope? You don't see this as a calamity? My future was with Brett! What hope can I have of ever moving on when I know I will never find anyone as wonderful as him again?*

She closed her eyes, hoping this was all just a horrible nightmare and that when she opened her eyes again she would be in Brett's arms, safe and sound. Mollie felt an arm wrap around her. *Could it be?* She opened her eyes to discover her dad standing next to her. She turned toward him and buried her head into his chest. Mollie needed to get out of there. As much as she wanted to be near Brett, she knew it was only his shell. His soul, what she loved most about him, was gone.

Mollie hated the fact that she was avoiding Brooke, but every time she saw Brooke with Derek it was like a knife being stabbed into her heart and then turned slowly. Mollie knew she was being selfish, but she couldn't fight the feelings of jealousy that welled up inside whenever she saw Brooke having the love of *her* life with her, supporting her, comforting her.

Back at the apartment, Mollie curled up on the couch. She still was not able to sleep in their bedroom, their bed. Mollie's landlord had heard about the accident and had graciously offered to move her into another apartment in the complex or release her from their lease. Mollie considered moving back in with her parents for a while, but she couldn't bear the thought of leaving her kindergarten class.

So, she decided to take the landlord up on the offer to move to another apartment. She wouldn't have to sign a new lease which meant that if she wanted to move back home, or somewhere else, she was free to do so as of July thirty-first. Part of her hated the idea of leaving the apartment that had been their home. But being there stirred up memories to the point that it was difficult to even breathe.

Each night, Mollie would fall asleep while watching their wedding video. Most people would think she was torturing herself. Yet, she found it almost therapeutic. By watching their video, Mollie could see Brett, hear him, remember his touch, his kiss. She would usually fall asleep dreaming of him; dreaming of their children, their future. It was waking up in the morning that was torture. With each new day came the realization that Brett was gone and that they would never have children together, never have a future. The only way Mollie knew how to cope was to pull the covers over her head and go back to sleep.

Normally, that is what she would have done but not today. Today was the funeral and as much as Mollie wanted to sleep it all away she couldn't. She needed to go. She needed a little closure. Her mom had been amazing these past few days. She was so understanding and yet Mollie could tell she was gently nudging her towards moving forward. Mollie loved that her mom said it that way, "Moving forward." Mollie would never "move on." She had come to terms with the fact that she would never fall in love again.

Most of the events of the funeral seemed to blur together. However, when Derek spoke on behalf of the family, his words captured Mollie's attention and brought her back to the week Brett spent with Mollie and Brooke after returning from Afghanistan. It was during that week that both Derek and Mollie met Brett for the first time.

"I only had the privilege of knowing Brett for a little over a year-and-a-half but, one of the memories that stands out in my mind is the first time I met him. You would have never known that we were strangers. From the moment we were introduced he made me feel like a long-lost friend. Brett had a way with people. He continually looked for ways to build others up. People would gravitate toward him, and I know in my heart that it is because he put his faith into action. He was such an example of the Greatest Commandment. He loved God and he loved people. But he didn't stop there. Many of you may not know this, but Brett had hopes of fulfilling the Great Commission too. He planned to go to seminary school to become a pastor and reach others for Christ. But Brett had another calling. He laid down his life for his wife. I will forever remember and honor this incredible man. Thank you."

What? Who told him about Brett wanting to be a pastor? And about him laying down his life for me? What will people say? Will they blame me for Brett's death? I know I do! I don't think I could take it if I knew others felt the same way, somehow judging me! Mollie slipped outside as soon as the service was done. She needed some air. Suddenly, she felt a hand on her shoulder. She spun around to see Brooke standing behind her.

"Hi," she said softly.

Mollie was thankful that Brooke hadn't asked, "How are you?" It was the question everyone seemed to ask and the one Mollie dreaded answering the most. Mollie noticed that Brooke looked tired. Her skin was pale and there were bags under her eyes. Mollie had been so wrapped up in her own self-pity that she hadn't even considered just how hard this has been on Brooke. Brett was her only brother, and Mollie had never seen a closer pair of siblings.

Mollie was at a loss for words. She put her arms around Brooke and they hugged for a long time. They didn't need to speak. Right now they just needed to lean on each other. Mollie felt Brooke's body shake as she began to cry. It was then that Mollie realized that she was crying too.

The burial ceremony had been more difficult than Mollie had anticipated, and she could tell that her body had done enough physical exertion for one day. Her heart? Well, her heart was so broken that she was amazed it was still beating.

CHAPTER SEVEN

It didn't take Blake long to realize just how much a person loses when in prison. Besides the obvious- his freedom- he had lost any sense of privacy. His pride was replaced with shame, and he no longer felt like he had any control. But there *was* something that prison gave him more of than he could handle and that was time, endless amounts of time to relive the awful decision that brought him there in the first place.

The past two weeks seemed like an eternity. The events of that day would play over and over in Blake's mind. Being fired, discovering his girlfriend was cheating on him and then…the accident. When Blake had left Abby's apartment he had come up with a plan. But nowhere in that plan had he contemplated the chance of someone else getting hurt. But his actions resulted in more than just someone getting hurt; he had killed someone. The gravity of knowing that he had taken someone's life and inflicted unbearable pain on the victim's family and friends made Blake wish that he had been the one who had died, not the other guy. *It should have been me!*

Blake's hearing was only a few hours away. *How can I face the friends and family of the man I killed? What could I possibly say or do to help alleviate some of their pain?* Blake knew they wouldn't be the only ones in the courtroom who were hurting. His parents planned to be at the hearing too.   Blake could still recall his father's words after the accident.

"Son, we love you. Only God can help us through something like this. We are praying for you constantly," he said, his voice trembling as he spoke.

In that moment, Blake realized how wrong he had been. His parents would not have judged him. If only he had called them when everything had fallen apart. Instead, Blake took matters into his own hands. And his plan...it backfired and now there was nothing he could do to right the wrong he had done.

As Blake waited to enter the courtroom, he felt anxiety building up inside him. But it wasn't the sentencing that made him anxious. He was already serving a life sentence; shackled by the guilt of his actions. No, Blake's anxiety came from the thought of seeing his victim's family and friends; seeing the sorrow on their faces over their loss and the rage they would have toward him, the man who so carelessly took the life of a hero.

In the courtroom, Brooke quietly waited with the others. In a matter of moments, the man who took Brett's life would walk through that door. *Will I instantly feel anger when I see him? Is he sorry for what he's done? Will I ever be able to forgive him?* Her thoughts were interrupted by the sound of the door opening. Brooke had painted a picture in her mind of what he would look like. But the man who was making his way across the courtroom looked nothing like what she had imagined. In an instant, she knew the answers to her questions.

Blake kept his head down as he walked into the courtroom. If he saw the others, especially his parents, he knew he would lose it. Blake sat quietly next to his court-appointed attorney. There was no need to hire one. He wasn't fighting the charges. Blake had pled guilty to vehicular manslaughter.

Minutes before the hearing, Blake's attorney told him about the plea bargain that had been reached with the District Attorney. Three years in prison with the possibility of early release, one year probation and a one thousand dollar fine. Blake would have been okay with whatever they had given him. The truth was that at least in prison he was surrounded by others who were living with the mistakes they'd made. They understood each other. But out there, in the real world, Blake would see the shame and sadness on the faces of his family and friends.

The judge read the sentencing and asked the bailiff to remove Blake from the courtroom. His attorney had been gracious enough to talk with the judge to arrange for Blake and his parents to meet in a conference room.

As soon as Blake's mom entered the room she threw her arms around him. He desperately wanted to hug her back, but the handcuffs wouldn't allow it. She hugged Blake hard, for a long time. Slowly, she stepped back and looked into his eyes. Blake noticed that she looked much older than the last time he saw her, and he knew it was because of him. The pain he had caused was taking its toll on both of his parents.

"We are praying for you son," she whispered, her voice trembling.

"I'm sorry Mom. I'm so sorry," he whispered, unable to fight back the tears.

"We know, honey, we know," she whispered as she gently stroked the back of his head. "Everyone makes mistakes. God loves you and forgives you and so do we," she said, displaying a calm that was missing just moments before. *How had I ever doubted them, doubted God? If only I had turned to them, to Him, when life had spiraled out of control!*

CHAPTER EIGHT

Both Karen and Brooke tried to talk Mollie into going to the hearing, but she wanted no part in it. She didn't want to put a face to the man who chose to drink and then got behind the wheel; the man who took her love, and her future, away from her. Besides, she needed to start packing, and she wanted some time alone while she went through Brett's things. She needed a fresh start but was still struggling with moving forward. She began to fear that, by moving, her memories of Brett would begin to fade.

Her thoughts wandered back to the phone call she received shortly after discovering that the other driver had been intoxicated. Mollie didn't recognize the number when it appeared on her cell phone.

"Hello?"

"Hello. Is this Mrs. Mollie Anne Walker?"

She instantly recalled where she had heard those words, that voice. It was the officer who had delivered the police report. *Why is he calling me? Have they discovered something new?*

"Yes. May I help you?" she asked.

"Ma'am. This is Officer Cooper. I delivered the police report regarding your accident. Ma'am, the reason I am calling is to apologize."

"Apologize? I...I don't understand," Mollie stammered.

"Ma'am, I am new to this position and am still learning protocol. I was supposed to deliver that report to the District Attorney, not you. I am so sorry that I subjected you to all that information without having someone with you to talk you through it. I hope you can forgive me," he said, trying his best to sound professional but Mollie could hear the remorse in his voice.

At first, she wasn't sure how to respond. She had been thankful to have some answers but being alone when she got those answers and then finding Brett's gift had almost sent her over the edge. Mollie assured him that everything was okay and that she appreciated his phone call.

"Ma'am, if you ever need anything, please don't hesitate to call," he added, a genuine warmth to his voice.

"I will. Thank you," she replied and hung up the phone. Mollie decided to save his phone number in her contacts just in case she needed more answers; just in case she needed someone to talk to.

A few days later, Mollie was finally feeling settled in the new apartment. There were still pictures and little mementos here and there, but it didn't feel as suffocating as it had in the other apartment, *their* apartment.

Mollie and her mom would go for long walks. The exercise helped strengthen her healing body. And her mom's constant nudging was paying off. Mollie was doing more around the apartment and was even running errands. It had been almost a month since the accident, and Karen had never left her side.

As days went by, Mollie began sensing it was time to get back to her students. She called her principal, Mrs. Higgins, to let her know that she planned to come back on Monday. Mollie's heart, and her eyes, overflowed when Mrs. Higgins told her that the other teachers had offered to cover her extra duties so she could gently work her way back into a routine.

It was bittersweet when it was time for Mollie to say goodbye to her mom. She didn't know how she would have made it through this without her mother by her side. Yet Mollie was anxious to get back to teaching and feel some sort of normalcy. The tears came easily and quietly as they said their goodbyes. Mollie walked her mom to her car and, right before she got in to leave, Karen handed Mollie a wrapped package.

"What's this?" Mollie asked, suddenly feeling awful that she had not thought to get her mother something.

"You'll see," Karen said, a smile appearing amid her tears.

Mollie gently opened the package. It was a book, a journal. On the cover was a beautiful picture of a path lined with huge trees that seemed to envelope it like an umbrella. Yet, despite the thickness of the trees' leaves, slivers of sunlight were gently cascading onto the path. Below the picture were these words, "Thy word is a lamp unto my feet, and a light unto my path. [4]" Mollie opened the book and discovered a note from her mom written on the first page.

> Mollie,
>
> I may not always be able to be with you but God and His Word are. I pray that these verses bring you the peace and comfort you need as you move forward and seek God in all you do. I love you with all my heart!
>
> "May the peace of God, which surpasses all understanding, guard your heart and your mind in Christ Jesus. [5]"
>
> Love,
> Mom

As Mollie turned the page she saw that some pages were tabbed. The tabs had labels like Trust, Love, Tragedy, Hope, Peace, Trials, Future, Grief, etc. She turned to the tab labeled Trust. There were several Scripture verses written on the page. Mollie read the first one. "Trust in the LORD with all your heart and lean not on your own understanding. [3]" Her tears began splashing onto the page. Mollie quickly wiped them away, not wanting anything to harm these sacred pages. Her mom had given her a spiritual first-aid kit. Mollie silently vowed to carry this with her always and turn to it when she needed to be filled with God's Word, His love.

"Thank you," she whispered.

Karen reached for her daughter and gave her a big hug. "There are blank pages in there for you to write in more Scripture as you walk with God," she said, stroking Mollie's hair and rocking her gently. "I love you honey," she whispered.

"I love you too," Mollie said as Karen got into her car and drove away.

Somehow, Mollie managed to get through the first week back at school. She had forgotten just how exhausting twenty kindergarteners could be. But she was thankful for the distraction. They kept her mind far from thoughts of Brett. It was at night, when Mollie's brain finally had a chance to recover, that memories of Brett would flood in. She longed to be in his arms, telling him about her day, sharing her life with him.

The help from the other teachers turned out to be more of a blessing than Mollie anticipated, especially when she discovered that the kindergarten team would be going on a field trip to the local Humane Society during her second week back. The squeals from the students could almost be heard over the barking of the dogs as they took their tour. Mollie couldn't help but notice the light in her students' eyes as they giggled and petted the animals. For the first time in a long time, she felt a smile, a real smile, come over her face.

The next day, Mollie's class was on a mission. After hearing the staff at the Humane Society talk about their need for supplies, her class wanted to send out fliers asking families for donations. Mollie was so proud of them. It reminded her of a verse she had recently added to the journal her mom gave her. "And do not neglect doing good and sharing; for with such sacrifices God is pleased.[6]"

By the end of the week, they had collected more than they could have hoped for. After school, Mollie loaded the items into her car and made the drive to the Humane Society.

Just inside the shelter's main doors is a large room. In front is the receptionist's desk and behind that are several offices that have been created using four foot high by eight foot wide partitions. Between two partitions sits a desk and some chairs. It is in these "offices" that adoptions take place. Mollie walked up to the receptionist.

"Hi. May I help you?" she asked pleasantly.

"Hi. My kindergarten class has collected donations and I was wondering where you would like me to put them," Mollie replied.

"Do you have a lot of items to drop off?" she asked.

"I do. It's amazing how much they collected," Mollie said, beaming with pride over her students and their accomplishment.

"Let me have someone help you." She turned around in her chair and called out, "Hey Steven. Would you be able to help bring in some donations?"

"Sure. I'll be right there."

Mollie looked up to see a man's face above the partitions. She immediately noticed how handsome he was; his jet black hair and the way his deep blue eyes lit up when he smiled. When he rounded the corner of the last office Mollie was finally able to see the rest of him. He was wearing an orange shirt and khaki pants.

They made their way out to Mollie's car, and she started handing him some of the items.

"Wow! This is all from you?" he asked.

"Actually, my kindergarten class came here for a tour and, after hearing about the needs of the animals, decided to send out fliers asking for donations. As you can see, they were very successful in their endeavor," she said, unable to stop smiling.

It wasn't until they had gathered all the items and were heading back into the building that she saw it. On the back of Steven's shirt, in bold, black letters was the word INMATE.

Had I been so pre-occupied with the students during our tour that I didn't notice that there were inmates working here? Not that it really matters. I guess it just took me by surprise, that's all.

Steven led Mollie over to a cart to place the donations on.

"Thank you for your help," she said, unable to keep her mind from wondering what this man could have possibly done to be an inmate.

"You are very welcome. You must be quite proud of your students," he said with a grin.

"I am. They love animals, just like their teacher," she replied, still unable to suppress her smile.

"Well, feel free to go on back and see the animals and let me know if you would like to take any of the dogs for a walk. They love to get outside in the fresh air. We even have a couple of fenced-in areas where you could let the dog off its leash to run."

"Thanks! I think I will go back there. And I'll definitely let you know if I want to walk any of them," Mollie added as she started heading toward the double doors that led to the animals.

"Wonderful!" he said with a smile and a wink, just like Brett used to do.

CHAPTER NINE

Mollie loved being with the animals at the shelter. They had such unconditional love and were desperate for someone to take them home and love them. She found herself visiting so often that it became part of her routine. Every Tuesday and Thursday after school she would make her way to the shelter.

And in no time, the staff began addressing her by name. She instantly clicked with Ruby, the new receptionist. Mollie could tell from her accent that she was from the South. She loved the way Ruby would refer to people as "Sugar, Honey or Dumplin'."

As weeks went by, Mollie learned a lot about the animals at the shelter. Many would be gone after only a week or two, but there were those who had been at the shelter for a long time. She was thankful that the Humane Society has a no kill policy. Nothing deserved to die simply because it wasn't wanted. Mollie started to include the animals at the shelter in her prayers at night. She prayed that somehow God would find a home for each of them.

Every night before she prayed, Mollie would talk to Brett. She would tell him how much she missed him and share stories from her day. She felt a peace knowing that he was in Heaven; hoping that he could hear her.

Mollie's prayers were full of requests for her family and friends, her students, the animals at the shelter and...him. It took her a while before she was able to bring herself to pray for Steven. She barely knew him. They had kept their conversations rather superficial, but there was something in his eyes, a sadness buried deep inside, that told Mollie she needed to pray for him. She wasn't sure quite what to pray for so she just asked God to be with Steven and to use her in any way that could help him. It was the same prayer she prayed for Brett when he was suffering from his flashbacks. *Why does this guy constantly remind me of Brett?*

W

It was Tuesday again and Mollie had just arrived at the shelter.

"Hi Ruby," she said as she made her way through the door.

"Well, hello there! How are you today, Sugar?" she asked.

"I'm doing pretty well. Say, I have a question." Mollie looked around to see if anyone could hear them.

Ruby got the hint and leaned forward, looking around too.

"What is it, Sugar?"

"Well, I have a question about...Steven," she whispered, praying no one could hear them.

"Oh, Honey! Isn't he a peach?"

"Shhhh! I don't want anyone to hear us," Mollie whispered.

"Oh...sorry Sugar," she whispered. "What's your question?"

"Well, what's...what's his story?" she asked.

"I wish I could tell you hon," Ruby replied.

"Oh," Mollie whispered, trying to hide her disappointment.

"Honey, I can't tell you because I don't know. You see, the work release program is to help prepare low-level criminals for the transition back into society once they have served their time. This place is kind of like a fresh start, a clean slate. The orange shirts are to make sure our patrons are aware of the situation but other than that, we try not to add any more labels than the one they wear on their backs. Besides, we know they are low-level criminals. It's not like any of them killed someone."

Those last words hit home. Mollie fought back the tears but she could feel them trying to break through.

"Oh Sugar! Have I said something to offend you?" Ruby exclaimed.

"No. I'm okay. I think I'll go see the animals. Thanks Ruby."

Mollie found Buster right away. He was Steven's favorite, and had quickly become her favorite too. Buster was a mutt but he had the sweetest disposition. He never seemed to get too excited about anything, and he loved to go for walks and play in the fenced-in area. Mollie could tell right away that Buster was smart. He had already learned several tricks in the few weeks she had been working with him. But she had a feeling that Steven had been working with him too.

Mollie hadn't seen Steven yet. It seemed a little odd. He was usually right by the double doors the moment she walked in. She was starting to think it was on purpose. It had happened too many times for it to be a coincidence.

As Mollie walked Buster, she replayed Ruby's words in her mind. "This place is a fresh start, a clean slate." *Why do I think I need to know his story?* A memory verse from Bible study instantly popped into her head. "If any of you lacks wisdom, you should ask God, who gives generously to all without finding fault, and it will be given to you.⁷"

Lately, Mollie had been praying for God's wisdom and the middle part of that verse sunk in when she thought about Steven. Jesus' sacrifice wipes the slate clean for all who confess and repent of their sins. *So, if God doesn't dwell on our faults, why should I?*

Suddenly, Mollie's thoughts were interrupted by Buster's barking. It startled her at first because she had never heard Buster bark like that before. They had walked quite a ways down a nearby dirt road and were making their way back to the shelter. Standing next to the shelter was Steven. Buster was pulling so hard on the leash, so excited to see Steven, that Mollie thought the leash would rip in two. She decided to jog a little so Buster could get to Steven faster.

As they got closer, Steven crouched down and Buster jumped on him. They both fell to the ground, Steven laughing and Buster covering him in kisses.

"Guess I won't need a shower tonight," he chuckled.

"Eww!" Mollie squealed, wrinkling her nose. "You're kidding, right?"

"Of course, silly. But they *do* say that dogs have the cleanest mouths," he replied with a smile and a wink.

"Have they smelled some of these dogs' breath? How can something so clean smell so horrid?" she asked, laughing.

"Point well taken," he said looking up at her. He started scratching Buster behind the ears. "What do you say big fella? Ready to go back inside? I think I might even have a treat for ya."

Mollie had heard of the theory about dogs *supposedly* having very clean mouths. Yet, she didn't quite believe it. However, she *does* believe in the theory that dogs have a certain sense when it comes to judging people. If that theory *is* true, that dogs can tell if someone is a good guy or not, then Steven was definitely a good guy. Not that Mollie needed a dog to tell her that. It was just nice to have a second opinion.

It wasn't until Mollie got home that she noticed how sore she was. She wondered if it was because of the jogging she did with Buster. Or, maybe she was sore from laughing with Steven. She had to admit that it felt good to run, to laugh, and that's when she realized what she should do. *Why didn't I think of this before?*

CHAPTER TEN

The next day, Mollie couldn't stop looking at the clock. As much as she loved being with her students, she couldn't wait for the last bell to ring. She needed to get to the shelter. And she could tell that Ruby was surprised to see her the moment she walked through the doors.

"Well, I'll be. What are you doing here on a Wednesday, Sugar?"

Mollie couldn't contain her excitement any longer. "I'm here to adopt Buster!"

"Well, praise Jesus! I was wondering when that old bag of bones was going to find a home," she chuckled.

Mollie looked for Steven as she made her way to the kennels. She couldn't find him anywhere. She quickly grabbed Buster's papers that hung in a plastic envelope on his kennel and made her way back to Ruby. They immediately started the adoption process and in less than half an hour Buster was hers. After a stop at the pet store for supplies, Mollie and Buster were finally home. Home. That was a word she hadn't used much since...

Having Buster gave Mollie an added sense of security, and she was thankful for his companionship. He seemed to feel right at home instantly. Mollie would stop by the apartment every day over her lunch break to let him out, and they went for walks every night. She missed going to the shelter and seeing Ruby...and Steven. But between work, Bible study and Buster, Mollie wasn't finding time to get there. She called to let Ruby know and asked her if she would let Steven know too. Mollie could hear the smile in Ruby's voice as she assured Mollie that she would. *Why on earth did I just do that? He probably hasn't even noticed that I haven't been by lately.*

A week had gone by and Mollie sensed that Buster missed Steven. There just seemed to be a little less spring in his step. So, she decided to call the shelter.

"Hey Ruby, it's Mollie."

"Well, hey there stranger! We sure have missed seeing you around here!"

We? Who is she referring to? "I was wondering if it would be okay to come by tomorrow after school for a visit."

"Sure Sugar! We would love to see you!" Ruby exclaimed.

There she goes again saying we! "Well, actually I was wondering if it would be okay to bring Buster with me. I wouldn't bring him in. I just thought that maybe Steven could come out to see him. I think Buster misses him," Mollie said, anxiously waiting for an answer.

"Oh, I see. *Buster* misses him," Ruby said with a hint of sarcasm.

Mollie could tell she was blushing. She didn't quite know how to respond. "Do you think it would be okay?" she asked again.

"I don't see why not! Let me double check though." There was a long pause. "The supervisor says its fine with him. I'll be sure to tell Steven right away tomorrow. I'm sure he will be excited to see *Buster*."

Is she hinting at something? Mollie shook her head. "Thanks Ruby! Can't wait to see you tomorrow!"

"See you tomorrow, Sugar!"

The next day, Mollie picked Buster up after school and drove to the shelter. The moment she pulled into the parking lot Buster started pacing in the back seat. Mollie wondered if Steven had been watching for them because he was already walking toward her car as she opened her door. "Hi!" he said as he approached.

Mollie suddenly felt nervous. "Hi," she replied and opened the back door to let Buster out.

Buster immediately leapt up and started licking Steven.

"Easy boy! It's good to see you too," he chuckled, trying to keep from falling to the ground.

Mollie grabbed a ball from the back seat, and they walked over to a grassy patch under a tree. They sat down and Steven started playing catch with Buster.

"He looks great," Steven said as he threw the ball.

"He's been amazing. We've started going for runs together. He is so calm and quiet in the apartment. The only problem is that he seems to miss you."

"You say that as if it's hard to believe," Steven chuckled.

Mollie gave his shoulder a little shove. "I did not," she replied, laughing.

He turned and looked at her. There was something about that look, something familiar. Mollie suddenly got nervous and looked away, pretending to watch Buster.

"I'm glad you came for a visit," he said, a gentleness in his voice.

"I realized it wasn't right for me to up and adopt Buster without telling you first. You really seem to care about him."

"I do care about...him," he said looking right into her eyes.

Mollie felt the blood instantly rush to her cheeks. *He said, "Him." Don't embarrass yourself Mollie.*

After several rounds of catch, Buster brought the ball back and laid down right between Steven and Mollie. They both began petting him. Mollie wasn't paying attention when suddenly her hand touched Steven's. A warm sensation came over her. She panicked and jerked her hand away. She could tell by the look on Steven's face that her actions had hurt him.

"Steven, I...I'm so sorry. It's not what you think," she stammered.

"Mollie, its okay. I understand," he said, keeping his eyes on Buster.

"Really, it's not....I...I recently lost a loved one and ever since I have been kind of jumpy. Really, that's all that was," she said, praying he would believe her.

44

"I'm so sorry for your loss," he said, a deep sorrow in his eyes like he had lost something, or someone, too.

They didn't speak for a while. Neither of them knew what to say. Eventually, it was time for Mollie to leave with Buster.

"This was fun," she said as she put Buster in the car. "We'll try to come again soon."

"I hope so. I would really like that," he said as he closed the car door for her.

The whole way home Mollie thought about that touch. *How could I possibly be getting so worked up over someone I barely know? That's an easy one to answer; I did the same thing when I met Brett.*

CHAPTER ELEVEN

As much as they enjoyed their visit to the shelter, Mollie knew that if she wanted Buster to know that he was with her now then she needed to gradually work Steven out of his life. So, she came up with a plan. They would visit Steven every other week, then eventually once a month and so on until Buster was weaned off of Steven. *Who am I kidding? Buster isn't the only one who needs this.*

Later that night, as Mollie sat in bed, Buster by her side, the events of the day played through her mind. *How could I have let someone into my heart so quickly?* She reached for the Scripture journal her mother had made for her. She turned to the first page and suddenly the verse from her mother's note sank in. "May the peace of God, which surpasses all understanding, guard your heart and your mind in Christ Jesus.[5]" Mollie's body may have healed from the accident, but her heart was still wounded, still vulnerable. *How could I have been so careless? I need to guard my heart.*

She began to wonder just how long it would take for her heart to heal. People have always complimented Mollie on her patience, especially with her students. But when it came to love, Mollie seemed to have little to no patience at all. *Hadn't God been faithful when Brett and I submitted to His will and timing? Why would I doubt Him now?*

The truth was that shortly before meeting Brett, Mollie had been feeling very alone. Brooke and Derek had been dating for several months and Mollie felt like the odd one out. Then Brett came for a week to visit Brooke. Mollie instantly developed very strong feelings for him but questioned whether those feelings were genuine or merely infatuation. Then, when Brett went back home and she didn't hear from him, she thought it meant that she needed to move on. She almost did.

One of the teachers at Mollie's school introduced Mollie to her son, Mitch. He showed interest in Mollie from the moment they met. He would call or text almost daily. It was nice to feel wanted. However, Mollie discovered that Mitch did not share the same beliefs as she did. She knew that it was better to be single than settle, especially when it came to faith. But when Brooke got engaged, Mollie almost called Mitch. She didn't want to be alone.

Only by the Grace of God was she able to stop herself from making that call. Right then and there she decided to put it all in God's hands and wait on His timing, not hers. She knew, deep down in her heart, that God's plan would far exceed anything she could envision. So when Brett surprised her less than a week later with a proposal on the Fourth of July, Mollie promised never to doubt again. *Oh, how quickly I can stumble!*

Mollie opened the drawer of her nightstand and pulled out a small black box. She opened it slowly, knowing that seeing this again would bring a rush of emotions. Shortly after the accident she had put it away. Perhaps because, like the apartment, it was a constant reminder of what she had lost. But now she needed it. She slipped it onto her finger as tears ran down her cheeks. It would still remind her of her loss but it would also be a constant reminder to give herself time, time to heal.

Mollie stared at her wedding ring. Instead of seeing just a ring, she saw a shield; something to protect her from unwanted advances. It had only been a couple of months since she last wore it, but it already felt foreign on her finger. How she longed for the days when it had felt awkward *without* it on.

Mollie found comfort in the thought that this ring would not only remind her of Brett but would help guard her heart. Suddenly, her mind started racing with questions. *What do I say if someone at Bible study notices it? What if Steven says something? Should I lie and say I'm engaged? That wouldn't be right. I should be honest with my Bible study group. But what about Steven? Do I share something so private with someone I barely know? Maybe I should take it off before each visit. It's not like we will be seeing each other much longer. Buster is already adjusting better to living with me and not seeing Steven as often. I wish I could say the same for me. Just more proof that I need to guard my heart.*

Mollie's thoughts were interrupted by something cold and wet touching her hand. It was Buster letting her know that it had been a while since she last petted him. Mollie had never had a dog before so she didn't really understand when people would say that dogs are man's best friend. But now that she had Buster, she completely understood. He had quickly become her best friend.

Mollie and Buster did practically everything together. She was thankful for his companionship, especially at night. He loved to snuggle up tight against her and having him there meant she wasn't all alone. But, as much as Mollie loved Buster, she would give anything for Brett to be there instead. Somehow, that wasn't *God's* plan, and she was still struggling to understand why.

Mollie desperately tried not to admit it, but she knew that she was angry with God. She couldn't understand why He would take Brett away from her, from this world, especially when he wanted to be a pastor. *Why would you take someone who wanted to dedicate his life to telling others about You? It just doesn't make sense.*

"Trust in the LORD with all your heart and lean not on your own understanding.[3]"

That verse had a way of popping into her head often. *We were putting our trust in You! I trusted You when I didn't know if I would ever find love. Brett trusted You when he felt the nudge to propose, even though it didn't make sense to those around us. We trusted You when You said we should save intimacy for marriage. All those times we trusted You and You showered us with blessings because of it. So why did this happen?*

Mollie turned to the Trials section of her Scripture Journal. She read each of the verses her mom had written. Then she noticed her own handwriting.

"Count it all joy, my brothers, when you meet trials of various kinds, for you know that the testing of your faith produces steadfastness. And let steadfastness have its full effect, that you may be perfect and complete, lacking in nothing.[8]"

Mollie remembered that first night of Bible study. She had never studied the book of James before and was anxious to see how God's Word would speak to her, especially after what had happened. In true God fashion, He spoke directly to her, right from the start. That verse was from their very first lesson and it took everything within her not to break down and cry as they talked about it within the group.

Several women shared about the trials they had been through or were currently going through. They ranged from addictions to illness to loss. God knew Mollie needed those words and that she needed these women to get through this. Yet, even with these demonstrations of God's love, Mollie still felt angry and hurt.

As weeks went by, the visits to the shelter became less and less frequent. Even though, in her head, Mollie knew that she would soon never see Steven again, she couldn't seem to get the message to her heart. She would get angry with herself when she noticed her heartbeat racing whenever she and Buster pulled into the shelter's parking lot.

These strange feelings towards Steven kept reminding her of Brett. When she questioned her initial feelings for Brett she was thankful for the chance to talk with her dad when he came down during Brett's visit to take everyone boating. Mollie and her dad rode together while Brett, Brooke and Derek drove separately. At first, Mollie was embarrassed when she discovered that her mom had told her dad about her feelings for Brett. But it turned out to be a blessing because it gave Mollie a chance to talk to her dad about relationships and how he knew that her mom was "the one."

He told Mollie about the first time he met Karen and how he was drawn to her confidence and character. She seemed different from the girls he had dated before. Some of his friends had gone on dates with Karen and she kind of "shot them down" when they tried to "put on the moves."

This intrigued her dad. So, he asked Karen out on a date. They met at a restaurant and ended up talking and laughing for hours. He found himself thinking about her all the time after their date and decided to call her and see if she wanted to go out again sometime. She agreed, and they met at a coffee shop a few days later.

Each time they went out they got to know more about each other. Mollie's dad said that by their third date he was smitten. He knew that she was the woman he wanted to marry and be the mother of his children.

They prayed about it and took the time to get to know each other instead of letting the physical cloud their judgment. So, Mollie took the initiative after that to get to know Brett, and the more she got to know him, the stronger her feelings for him became.

But with Steven it was different. She barely knew him and yet, somehow, he had found a way into her heart. The only explanation Mollie could come up with is that her heart was broken and empty; desperate to find someone to make it whole again. That had to be it.

CHAPTER TWELVE

It had been months since the accident and Blake thought that by now he would be used to being in prison, but he was wrong. Each passing day became more and more bleak. The only rays of light were his job and those visits. Getting out of those concrete walls, if only for a few days a week, felt like Heaven. And the visits...he never imagined someone showing him such kindness, such compassion. It was renewing his faith in people and, more importantly, in God.

Blake began reading the Bible daily. The more he drew closer to God, the more he could feel a change taking place within him. Blake sensed that those around him noticed too. Somehow God hadn't given up on him. So, he wasn't going to give up on God. Not after He put her in his life...

It had been over a month since Brooke saw Mollie at the funeral and so much had happened since then. Brooke hated the fact that she was keeping secrets from Mollie, but she didn't know how Mollie would react. *Will she understand? Will she be angry?* Brooke prayed every night for God to give her wisdom. *How do I tell her? How can I make her understand?*

With each passing day, Mollie was getting closer to the end of the school year and the big decision she had to make. *Should I stay*

and teach another year? Should I move back home to be closer to family? Or, should I up and move somewhere new and truly make a fresh start? Mollie had been mentally weighing the pros and cons of each option and still wasn't able to make a decision.

It was Friday and although most people look forward to the weekend, Mollie dreaded it. Without the demands of teaching she had more time to think; to remember all that she once had, all that she had lost. As Mollie gathered up her things to go home she suddenly remembered that Brooke would be in town visiting her parents. Mollie decided that after her walk with Buster she would call Brooke and see if they could come over for a visit. Mollie was just about to walk out of her classroom when she was startled by the sound of her principal's voice over her intercom.

"Mollie? Are you there?"

"Yes, Mrs. Higgins. Is something wrong?" she asked.

"Could you please come down to my office right away?" she requested, a hint of concern in her voice.

Mollie quickly made her way down the hall. Mrs. Higgins hadn't answered her question. *Is something wrong?* Mollie's mind tried to think of possible reasons for being called to the office, but she was drawing a blank. As she entered Mrs. Higgins' office, she was directed to a chair. What Mrs. Higgins told Mollie made her heart, and her stomach, ache.

"Oh no! Is he okay?" Mollie asked, trying to keep her emotions under control.

"He's okay. A neighbor happened to come home early and noticed him sitting by his front door. She called his parents right away and had Matthew stay with her until they got home. Luckily, it is April so it wasn't very cold out."

"But, what if he had wandered off or what if someone had taken him! I can't believe I forgot!" Mollie sobbed.

Mrs. Higgins waited patiently as Mollie regained her composure.

"He...he gave me a note this morning. He was supposed to go to the afterschool program and not ride the bus home. When I saw the note I was sure I would remember when it was time to leave.

But, with all that goes on during the day, it must have slipped my mind! How could I have been so careless?" Mollie said, trying to fight back the tears welling up once again.

"Mollie, we are human. Mistakes are bound to happen, and this could have happened to any one of us," Mrs. Higgins added, a gentleness in her voice.

"I...I need to call his parents. I need to apologize," Mollie stammered.

"I spoke with Matthew's parents. As you can imagine, they had the same scenarios run through their minds as you just did. And although they are very thankful that everything turned out okay and he is now in his home, safe and sound, they are very upset that this happened. I think it would be a good idea for you to call them and apologize."

"I'll go do it right now!" Mollie said as she jumped out of the chair.

Mollie's hands trembled as she dialed the number. *Lord, please give me the strength and the words to get through this.* Matthew's mother answered the phone. Mollie could hear the strain in her voice; that she had been crying.

"Hello."

"Hello. Is this Mrs. Tate?" Mollie asked, her voice trembling.

"This is."

"Mrs. Tate, this is Mrs. Walker..." Mollie was caught off guard by her words...*Mrs. Walker.* Her pause gave Mrs. Tate an opportunity to speak.

"What do you have to say for yourself?" she hissed.

Mollie was so shocked that she couldn't breathe. *She is furious with me! What do I say?*

"Mrs. Tate I am so sorry! Matthew showed me the note this morning and I must have forgotten when it was time to leave. I am so sorry. I promise it will never happen again!" Mollie's voice trembling uncontrollably now.

"Don't make promises you can't keep! I asked to have Matthew put in another classroom, but he loves having you for a teacher and

53

Mrs. Higgins said it would be better for him to stay in your class since it is so close to the end of the school year," she said, her voice, and her anger, rising with each word.

She wanted him moved to another class! Mollie was going to speak, but Mrs. Tate continued.

"I plan on emailing Mrs. Higgins every day to let her know where Matthew needs to be. I will email you too, but I don't expect you to remember," she said, her words cutting deeper and deeper.

Mollie wanted to tell her side of the story, to explain to Mrs. Tate that it would not happen again but, instead, she simply replied, "I understand, Mrs. Tate. I am so very sorry. Will you please tell Matthew how sorry I am?"

"If I can remember," she said and hung up.

That's when Mollie lost it. She put her head on her desk and sobbed. *It was an accident! I would never intentionally do anything to hurt someone, especially one of my students! Why doesn't she understand? Why can't she accept my apology? Will she ever forgive me?*

Mollie sat there for a long time, letting her emotions have their way with her. *What time is it?* She looked up at the clock. It was 5:30. *Buster!* Somehow amid the never-ending tears, Mollie drove to the apartment. She and Buster quickly made their way to the walking path. Mollie knew how much Buster liked long walks but that just wasn't going to happen today. No. He would have to do his business, and then they would head straight to the car.

CHAPTER THIRTEEN

Mollie fought back tears as she drove to her in-laws. Her mind drifted back to the day she met Brooke. Mollie had been anxious about starting college and having a roommate, especially someone she had never met. But as soon as Mollie walked into her dorm room and saw Brooke she felt an instant connection, and the two have been best friends ever since. They lived together on campus and even for a couple years after graduating, until they both got married.

They were as close as sisters. So, when Brett and Mollie got married, it simply made it more official. Mollie knew Brooke would be surprised to see her, but she didn't expect the reaction she got when Brooke opened the door. Mollie had always been able to read Brooke, but tonight she couldn't figure out why Brooke looked so nervous.

Brooke could tell right away that Mollie had been crying.

"Mollie, what's wrong?"

"I...I need to...to talk," Mollie said between sobs.

"Come in," Brooke said as she held the door open. Her eyes were so kind, so concerned.

"But, Buster..."

"Bring him in. My parents won't mind. Besides, I am the only one here right now," she said as she placed a hand on Mollie's arm.

Mollie quickly went back to her car and got Buster.

They walked toward the living room and sat down on the couch. Buster jumped up onto Mollie's lap, trying to comfort her.

Brooke looked deep into Mollie's eyes, searching for some sort of answer. "Mollie, what happened?" she asked.

"I...I accidentally sent a student home and...and the parents are furious with me! They want him put in...another class!" Mollie wailed.

Brooke was trying to put the pieces together. "Is he okay?" she asked gently.

"Yes...a... neighbor came home and saw him. But, but the mom...she...she...hates me!"

Brooke put her hand on Mollie's shoulder. "Mollie, I am sure she doesn't hate you. She is just really upset right now. People tend to say things they regret when they are upset. I'm sure that, in time, she will forgive you."

"But...but you didn't hear the way she talked to me! She hates me and...I tried to apologize but she...she hung up on me!" Mollie buried her head in her hands.

Brooke put her arms around Mollie, and they sat there for a moment. Mollie missed the feeling of someone's arms around her. She missed Brett more than ever.

It broke Brooke's heart to see Mollie so wounded. *She has been through so much and now this?* Brooke could only imagine what that mother must be feeling, but she hated to see her friend so upset. It had been an accident. Mollie would never hurt anyone.

Brooke had planned on telling Mollie everything this weekend but, with Mollie so upset now wasn't the right time. Brooke would just have to wait a little longer and pray that God would give her the wisdom to know when it was the right time. For now, like Brooke had done ever since the funeral, she would put the focus on Mollie and her needs. Eventually, when the time was right, Mollie would know the truth.

After a while, Mollie composed herself. It was then that she saw the tears in Brooke's eyes. Seeing how much Brooke cared about her brought a new set of tears to the surface.

Mollie was thankful for their friendship and that they could tell each other everything. But lately Mollie couldn't shake the feeling that Brooke was keeping something from her. Anytime they talked or texted it always seemed to be about Mollie. Whenever Mollie asked Brooke about work or Derek, her answers were always short and to the point. *Is something wrong?*

Brooke squeezed Mollie's hand. "Mollie, I believe that one day that woman will forgive you."

Tears came rushing in. "Brooke, you didn't hear her. It wasn't just her words. There was pure hatred in her voice. It's impossible."

"*Nothing* is impossible with God,[9]" she said, gently squeezing Mollie's hand again. "And I believe that one day *you* will be able to forgive too," she added, her eyes glistening.

"Forgive *her*?" Mollie asked, confused.

"No," Brooke said, pausing to let her words sink in a little deeper.

"Forgive *him*? *Never!*" Mollie shrieked, surprised by the rage in her voice.

"Mollie, he may be the one in prison, but you are the real prisoner if you continue to harbor this anger and unforgiveness. I'm not saying that it is going to happen today, but my prayer is that one day you will be able to forgive him. Think of how that woman's unforgiveness and anger toward you is making you feel. Now imagine what he must be going through," she said, trying to be as delicate as possible, knowing full well that these were things that Mollie did *not* want to hear.

"Imagine what *he* must be going through? You must be joking! I don't *care* what he is going through. What about what *I* am going through, huh? He took Brett away from *me*, from *us*. He deserves what he got. How could you possibly compare what I am going through to him?" Mollie knew her words were strong, but she didn't care.

"Mollie, I understand that, to you, there is no comparison. His actions versus yours don't even come close. But God doesn't rank sin. To Him, sin is sin. All of us mess up. None of us deserves forgiveness. But because of God's immense love for us, He freely offers forgiveness no matter what we have done, as long as we repent and ask for forgiveness."

"So, now *I'm* the bad guy?" Mollie barked.

"No. You're human. I had these same feelings toward him. It wasn't until I went to the hearing and saw him, saw the sorrow in his eyes. I started to wonder if I was really honoring Brett by withholding mercy from this man. The answer was no. And, what was worse, I wasn't honoring God either."

"So you've forgiven him?" Mollie was in utter disbelief.

"It took a while. I prayed about it for a very long time."

"How do you know he wasn't just putting on a good show? Maybe he thought that if he looked remorseful the judge would go easy on him?"

"Actually, he pled guilty and the DA and his lawyer had already come to an agreement before the hearing began." Something about the look on Brooke's face gave Mollie the feeling that there was something Brooke wasn't telling her.

"Still, how can you know for sure?" Mollie asked, not expecting an answer.

"Well, I trust God and..." Brooke hesitated.

"And what, Brooke? I know you are keeping something from me. What is it?" Mollie demanded.

"I've been...visiting him," she said softly, unable to look Mollie in the eyes.

"You've what? You've been *visiting him*!" Mollie wasn't sure if it was shock or anger that had paralyzed her.

"I'm so sorry Mollie. I should have told you right away but I didn't know how. I was afraid you would be angry with me. So, I kept praying that God would show me when it was the right time to tell you. My hope and prayer has been that God would soften your heart so that you would want to forgive him too."

"Never! Obviously, it is *your* choice if you want to forgive him but I can't, I *won't*!"

"Mollie, it was an accident..."

"No it *wasn't*! I *hate* that everyone calls it that. It was *not* an accident! He *chose* to drink and then got behind the wheel. The police report said he may have been drinking when he hit us! I could have forgiven him if it had been a stroke or a seizure, something that was out of his control. But what he did was totally preventable. I will never forgive him!"

Brooke looked at Mollie for a moment, tears streaming down her cheeks. "I'm sorry. I shouldn't have told you. Not tonight after all you have just been through."

Mollie felt her shoulders drop. She had never spoken to Brooke like that before. A verse from her Bible study immediately came to her mind, "...be quick to listen, slow to speak and slow to become angry.[10]" She had done the opposite and the effects of her actions, and her words, were written all over Brooke's face.

"I'm sorry too. I shouldn't have spoken to you like that," Mollie said, desperately trying not to cry.

Brooke reached out and hugged her. Mollie felt Brooke's body shake as she cried. *How could I have treated her this way?* Brooke pulled back and looked into Mollie's eyes.

"Mollie, I only said those things to you because I care about you. It hurts me to see you in so much pain. Ever since I forgave Blake I have had this peace that I never imagined having after losing Brett. I just want the same for you. He really is sorry about what happened. He's even started reading the Bible and is learning more every day about God and the gift of salvation through Jesus. There are times when I think I should stop visiting him. But then I wonder if my visits are somehow helping him come to Christ."

Even though Mollie wasn't ready to admit it, she knew that Brooke was right. Mollie needed to hear those words. She knew she was punishing herself by not forgiving him, but she just wasn't ready yet. Her emotions were waging a war against her, and she was ashamed to admit that they were winning. Maybe, one day, she would be ready to forgive. Mollie asked Brooke to continue praying for her; to pray that God would continue to heal her heart and give her the strength to fight these feelings of anger, guilt, depression and fear that had taken a hold of her.

Little did Mollie know that jealousy was waiting in the wings, ready to join the others. She was in for the fight of her life.

CHAPTER FOURTEEN

It was getting late when Mollie and Brooke heard the front door open. It was Derek. Brooke was sure that their tear stained faces had his mind racing. But instead of firing away with questions he simply said hello and went over to give Mollie a hug. Tears immediately gathered again in Brooke's eyes. *Oh how I love that man! How I wish Brett was still here for Mollie!*

Brooke couldn't begin to imagine what Mollie has been going through. *Why did I tell her about the visits? Have I gotten ahead of God or was now really the right time to tell her? Lord, please be with her. She needs you.*

Ever since Mollie told her about adopting Buster, Brooke had been praying that the dog would give Mollie a sense of security and be the companion she needed, especially now. After meeting Buster, Brooke knew right away that her prayers had been answered.

The hug from Derek rattled Mollie. Other than her father, Mollie has not had the arms of a man wrapped around her, not since... The strength of Derek's embrace, the smell of his cologne, were all reminders of Brett. It took every ounce of strength not to cry. Mollie knew it was time to leave. She was worn out, in every sense of the word.

Together, they made their way to the front door. Derek had his arm around Brooke's waist as they talked a while longer in the entryway. Both Derek and Brooke hugged Mollie and suggested going out to lunch the next day. Mollie tried to think of an excuse as to why she couldn't go, but her brain was exhausted. The truth was that seeing them together, Derek's arm around Brooke, stirred up an intense feeling of jealousy. *Why can't I have that? Why did my husband have to die? Why do I have to be alone? Why God, why?*

Brooke bent down to say goodbye to Buster. Suddenly, he lunged toward Brooke's face and she realized that she had made a huge mistake. Mollie was already opening the front door when she heard a gasp. She turned around just as Brooke ran toward the hallway.

CHAPTER FIFTEEN

"Oh no! What happened?" Mollie exclaimed.

"It's okay. Buster just gave Brooke a kiss goodbye," Derek replied, desperately trying to mask his nervousness.

In the silence of the moment, Mollie could hear the toilet in the hall bathroom flush. Slowly, her mind was putting the pieces together.

Mollie instantly turned toward Derek. She could tell by the look on his face that he was trying to think of something to say. Mollie didn't wait for him to speak.

"Is she...is she *pregnant*?" Mollie asked, waiting for Derek to laugh and tell her how silly she was.

He was about to answer when Brooke returned. Her face was pale. "Are you pregnant?" Mollie asked impatiently.

"I am," she said quietly. Mollie could see in Brooke's eyes that she was sorry for having her find out like this.

"How long?" Mollie asked, still trying to process the information.

"I found out shortly after the funeral. January had been such a hectic time at the hospital. They were short nurses so I had to work extra shifts. I guess I totally forgot about 'that time of the month.' Then, when I started not feeling well and seemed to tire easily I thought it was because of the...because of losing Brett. Once things settled down after the funeral I went to the calendar to see when my next 'time' would be and realized I hadn't written anything down in January. So, I took a test and it came back positive. Mollie, I should have told you right away. It's just that...after Brett's letter I didn't know how to tell you. I thought that if I waited that time would help heal your heart. This isn't how I intended for you to find out! I thought my 'morning sickness' was finally getting under control. But one lick from Buster, and his dog breath brought it right back. Mollie, I am so sorry!"

Mollie couldn't believe she was still standing. She thought losing Brett had brought her close to the breaking point, but now she was starting to think she was wrong. Her head and her heart were racing. She felt numb. This was all too much.

"I've got to go," Mollie said as she walked out the door. She couldn't be there anymore. She needed to get home. Seeing Brooke and Derek together was hard enough. But now, knowing that they had a child on the way, something Mollie would never get to share with Brett, was more than she could take.

As Mollie stormed out the front door she could hear Brooke crying and calling out her name but she kept walking. She wouldn't look back. She needed to get home.

Brooke spent most of the weekend crying. Other than the day after the accident and the funeral, she had never seen Mollie look so hurt, so alone. Knowing that she was the one to make Mollie feel that way was killing her. Derek and her parents kept trying to reassure her that, in time, Mollie would forgive her, but it still didn't take away the guilt she was feeling. *How could I have kept these things from her?*

Over the past few months, Brooke had hoped to gradually tell Mollie about the visits and the pregnancy. Instead, both bombs were dropped in a matter of minutes, and Brooke could tell that the damage was extensive. She wanted to go to Mollie, to apologize. But Brooke knew that Mollie wasn't ready to hear it. She had been avoiding Brooke's calls all weekend and hadn't responded to any of her texts. At least Mollie had Buster. Knowing that she wasn't completely alone gave Brooke *some* comfort.

And even though so much had been revealed that night there was still one very important piece of information left unsaid. Brooke didn't want to be the one to tell Mollie. Perhaps Derek could do it. All Brooke could do was pray that Mollie would have an open heart, and mind, when she finds out...

CHAPTER SIXTEEN

Other than walks with Buster and a trip to the grocery store, Mollie spent the rest of the weekend in bed. She didn't want to see or talk to anyone. She didn't know what she would have done if she hadn't had Buster there by her side. When he would look at her with those sweet puppy dog eyes it was as if he understood.

By Monday, Mollie started to feel a little better. She thought about calling in sick, but that would mean spending another day at home with nothing but time to think about all that had just happened. She needed something to take her mind off of it, and her students would definitely do that.

As her students began filing into the classroom, they bombarded her with stories about their weekend. It was just what Mollie needed. It wasn't until she began taking attendance that she realized that Matthew Tate was absent. Her heart sank. She desperately fought back the tears that were coming to the surface.

During the next few hours Mollie tried to keep her focus on the other students, but she found her mind wandering constantly. *Did his mother pull him out of the school? Is she still that angry with me? Lord, please help me!*

Finally, it was time for recess. She wanted to run to Mrs. Higgins' office to see if she knew anything, but Mollie had recess duty. Behind her sunglasses she let the tears come. Suddenly, she felt a light tap on her hip.

Mollie spun around and there was Matthew! Her heart leapt with joy. She bent down and gave him a huge hug.

"My mom said we had a rough morning. Sorry I'm late."

Mollie put her sunglasses on the top of her head so she could look him in the eyes.

"Ms. Mollie, you're crying," he said, a look of concern quickly appearing on his face.

Mollie smiled. "These are good tears. It's because I am so happy to see you!   Matthew, I am so sorry that I sent you home last Friday. I made a mistake and I will never let it happen again. I hope you can forgive me," the gravity of her request suddenly sinking in.

"Of course I forgive you," he squealed as he gave her a big hug. And with that, he ran off to play with the others.

Mollie was struck by how quickly and completely he had forgiven her. Children don't hold grudges. They forgive and move on. Maybe Brooke was right. Maybe Mollie was somehow punishing herself by harboring this anger and unforgiveness. *Can I really forgive the man who took Brett away from me?* She realized that *she* couldn't. But with *God's* help, maybe she could. *Lord, please help me be able to forgive! I can't live like this much longer.*

Mollie knew what she needed to do. She needed to talk to someone. Normally, she would turn to Brooke, but she wasn't ready for that, not yet. Mollie knew she was being stubborn, but the emotional wounds from Brooke's secrecy were still too fresh. Maybe Brooke really had been waiting until the right time to tell her; to break the news gently. But they had *never* kept secrets from each other. Mollie's sense of trust had been shaken.

As soon as school was done, Mollie picked up Buster and drove straight to the shelter. As she sat in the parking lot she said a quick prayer. "Lord, please give me the strength to do this. Please guide my heart and my words. Amen."

Buster and Mollie walked up to the front door.

"Well, hey there Sugar! I wasn't expecting to see you so soon!"

Mollie could always count on a warm welcome and a smile from Ruby. "Hi Ruby. I know we weren't planning to see each other until tonight but I just had to come here. Is Steven around?"

"Sorry hon. He doesn't come on Mondays," Ruby replied.

Mollie could tell by the look on Ruby's face that she was concerned.

"Would you be able to go for a little walk?" Mollie asked, her eyes begging Ruby to say yes.

"Right now tends to be our slow time. I can probably get away for about fifteen minutes."

Mollie could tell that Ruby was curious as to what was so important that they needed to talk now instead of waiting until Bible study. As soon as they stepped out of the front door, Mollie started talking. She had so much to tell Ruby and only fifteen minutes. Mollie told her about the night Brett died, about the necklace she had given him before they were engaged and how she became angry with God when she saw Brett wearing it at the funeral. She showed Ruby the necklace Brett had made just for her. She explained why she visited the shelter so often; that it was one of the few places where she has found joy during her time of grief. She told Ruby about finding out that Brooke has been visiting the man who killed Brett and that Brooke is pregnant. Mollie shared with her how hurt she was that her best friend had kept such secrets from her. By the time they started walking back to the shelter, Mollie was in tears.

Ruby took Mollie's hand. Instead of a look of shock on her face, there was a look of empathy, of understanding. "Sugar, we need to talk some more but I can't right now. Would you be able to come early to Bible study tonight?"

"Of course. What time?"

"How about six. I'll meet you in the church lobby," she said, giving Mollie's hand a little squeeze.

"Okay. See you then," Mollie replied as they stopped by her car. Ruby gave her a big hug and walked back toward the shelter.

Mollie was stunned. She thought Ruby's head would be spinning. Instead, there was a calm about her. Hopefully the next couple of hours would go by quickly. Mollie was eager to talk with Ruby again. She wanted to hear what Ruby had to say.

Ruby watched as Mollie drove off. *Lord, that young girl has been through so much. She reminds me of me.*

Ever since the day Ruby met Mollie, she felt a sort of connection to her. Initially, she thought it was their common faith and was thrilled when Mollie invited her to a Monday night women's Bible study. But now, after listening to Mollie's story, Ruby began to see that their connection was much deeper than she first thought.

Ruby and her husband had just moved to the area, and she was thankful to find a friend in Mollie. And it was nice to meet other women, especially women of faith, through their Bible study group. Ruby had been tempted to share her story when their lesson was about the trials we face. James 1:2-3 were verses she knew by heart not so very long ago. "Consider it pure joy, my brothers and sisters, whenever you face trials of many kinds, because you know that the testing of your faith produces perseverance.[11]" Ruby would be the first one to admit that the trial she and her husband went through was the furthest thing from joy. It almost destroyed them.

There are still days when Ruby wants to ask God, "Why?" But if she dwells on it too long, then all the pain and anger from the past resurfaces. She and her husband have worked too hard to go back there. Only by the grace of God are they still together. And only by the grace of God are they both still alive. Although Ruby was concerned about how Mollie might react to her story, she had a feeling that somehow it might help her.

CHAPTER SEVENTEEN

It wasn't until Mollie got home that she realized that her weekend of sulking had kept her from finishing her Bible study lesson. She feverishly began working on it and was somehow able to push everything else out of her mind and focus on God's Word. The lesson was over the fourth chapter of James. Two things stuck out immediately: coveting and pride.

Mollie *knew* she was jealous of Brooke being pregnant. And, she *knew* that she was being stubborn and prideful by not returning Brooke's calls or texts, but she was still hurting. Mollie was fighting with her emotions and felt weak and defeated. Most days she felt so lost that she didn't know what to do. *Maybe I should be asking God for wisdom, just like it says in James 1:5. Maybe God will speak to me through Ruby.*

Mollie managed to finish her lesson and get to the church in time. She glanced at her phone. It was ten to six. She looked out into the church parking lot and could barely contain her excitement as she saw Ruby pull in.

As soon as Ruby pulled into the parking lot she saw Mollie getting out of her car. *Lord, please speak through me and give me the strength to tell my story. It has been awhile, and I won't be able to get through it without You.*

Ruby could tell by the look on Mollie's face that she was anxious to continue their talk. Ruby wanted some privacy so she pointed over toward a couch that was off to the side, tucked away from the lobby. She took a deep breath as she pulled out a piece of paper. She had so much to tell Mollie. As Ruby stared down at her notes her hands began to tremble.

"Sugar, there is something I want to tell you. No one here knows about this, and I would like this to stay between you and me," she said, her voice beginning to waver.

"Of course," Mollie replied, her eyes full of concern.

"A few years ago my husband and I had a son. His nickname was Junior because he was named after my husband James. He was so precious and we both instantly fell in love with him. It had taken us quite a while to get pregnant, but we were finally a family. I treasured the weeks I had with Junior during my maternity leave.

"I gradually eased my way back to work. I began working only a couple of days a week and then added on until I was back full time. We had found a wonderful daycare center, which made it a little easier to be away from him.

"One morning I needed to be at the office early for a meeting, so James offered to take Junior to daycare. I was thankful for his help. I knew James would be leaving right behind me so I offered to put Junior in his car. I placed Junior in his carrier and buckled him in the back seat. Then I kissed him on the head, told him that his mommy loves him very much and rushed to my car.

"Work had been busy and I was thrilled to finally be on my way to pick up Junior. I walked into the center, and the look on the director's face immediately sent up a red flag. Instead of greeting me with a smile she had a confused look on her face. When I asked if Junior had a good day her look turned to absolute horror. She said that Junior was not there. The room started to spin. She could tell I was about to faint and rushed to my side. I asked her if James had already picked him up. That's when she told me that Junior had not been there all day.

"By this point I was on the floor, praying that there had been a mistake. My hands trembled uncontrollably as I called James. He answered and I immediately asked him where Junior was. There was a pause and then I heard James bellow, 'No!' I could hear him running and then the sound of banging and moaning. I had never heard those sounds come out of him before. I wanted to know what was happening. I kept yelling for him to tell me what was going on.

"Someone must have heard James and taken the phone. By then I was screaming. Finally, the person on the other line told me what I was dreading. Junior was dead."

Ruby could feel the sobs rising up within her but she needed to finish. She needed Mollie to hear it all.

"I must have passed out because the next thing I remember was being in a hospital, my sister by my side. Slowly, she shared with me what had happened. That morning James was about to go out to his car when he accidentally spilled coffee all over himself. He ran back inside and changed clothes but by the time he got into his car he was running late for work. With all the distractions, he had forgotten about dropping Junior off at daycare. It wasn't until I called that James realized what had happened. Junior had been in the car the whole time and had died from heatstroke.

"I went to stay with my sister. I couldn't bear to be around James. I felt as if my world had come crashing in all around me. My doctor prescribed some pills to help me sleep. I started taking them regularly so that all I did was sleep. If I was awake my mind would replay the events of that day over and over again. I was devastated. And, I was furious. I was angry at myself for not taking Junior to daycare. I was angry at the director for not calling me when Junior wasn't dropped off. I was angry at James for leaving our beautiful boy in the car. And I was angry at God. I kept asking Him why He would allow something like this to happen. There were times when I thought about taking all my pills at once so I could be with Junior. I didn't want to live without him.

"Seeing Junior at the visitation was excruciating. I wanted to hold him, to see his smile and the light in his eyes. But that would never happen. My angel was gone and my heart was broken. I buried my head in my hands. Suddenly, I heard a noise and looked up to see James beside me. I wanted to hit him. I wanted to hurt him like he hurt me. My emotions were raging inside me and I was ready to attack. Just then he fell to the ground and began sobbing.

He asked me if I could ever forgive him. Immediately my mind screamed, 'No!' But, only by the grace of God did I pause. I looked at him. I realized that there was no need to hurt him. His pain was greater than mine. But how could I ever forgive him? Junior was dead because of him.

"I felt my whole body grow hot. Anger was creeping into every part of me. I was ready to unleash all that I was feeling. James kept saying, 'I'm so sorry. I can't lose you too. Please forgive me.' But I didn't feel like forgiving him. I felt like punishing him. Just as I was about to fire away with my words I looked back at Junior and saw a cross sewn into the inside of the lid of the casket. That's when it hit me. Forgiveness isn't a feeling, it's an action. I'm sure Jesus didn't *feel* like suffering and dying on the cross, but He did it anyway because He loves us so much.

"So, even though I didn't *feel* like it, I placed my hand on James' shoulder and told him I forgave him. He leapt up and threw his arms around me. Instead of feeling the weight of his embrace I felt as if a weight was being lifted *off* my shoulders. We wept together for several minutes. For the first time I felt like we might make it through this, that the worst was over. But I was wrong."

CHAPTER EIGHTEEN

Mollie was stunned. As she listened to Ruby's words she tried
to empathize. Ever since Brett's death, Mollie has felt incomplete;
like a part of her died with him. But...to lose a child? How could
she possibly understand what Ruby has been through? And, not
only did Ruby lose her only child but at the hands of her husband. It
had been an accident. There was no doubt about it. But how could
she ever get past that? At least the man who took Brett's life was a
stranger, some faceless person Mollie will probably never meet.
She had a target for her anger and hurt. But Ruby... how could she
ever love someone who has caused her such pain, such loss?
Mollie reached for her hand.

W

"After the funeral I continued to stay with my sister. I still
needed time to heal, and I wasn't ready to see Junior's things
around the house, his crib forever empty. With all that I was
dealing with I knew that James was having more difficulty coming to
terms with what had happened. He didn't even tell me that he had
been charged with murder. Shortly before his court date, the
charge was reduced to involuntary manslaughter, child abuse and
neglect.

"I had just lost my son and now I could possibly lose my
husband. I felt as if I couldn't breathe, couldn't move. Only by the
grace of our Heavenly Father was I able to summon the strength to
testify on James' behalf. I was still angry with him but knew in my
heart that it had been an accident. I also knew that he would spend

the rest of his life haunted with unimaginable guilt. He didn't deserve to go to prison too. Because of my testimony, eye witness accounts and the audio recordings from the 911 call, the judge dismissed all of the charges.

"We thanked God for delivering James from those charges. When the judge told James that he was free to go, the comment resonated through me. He was free to go but we would never be free from our pain. I was so consumed with my own feelings that I totally neglected his. My sister saw how much we were both suffering and suggested that we each go to a Christian counselor.

"James found a male counselor and I started seeing a female one. At first I was leery about sharing all of my thoughts and feelings. Eventually, after several visits, they started pouring out. I couldn't hold it in any longer. There were moments when I was disgusted with what I was saying, but I had such anger raging within me. My counselor spent most of our time together listening. This continued for several weeks. Finally, I came to a point when I had nothing left to say.

"She asked about my encounters with James. I told her that when we saw each other at the visitation that I was able to tell him I forgave him and that, initially, I felt a peace come over me. Then I admitted that, since that day, I have had countless moments of anger and resentment toward him and have used my words to convey my hurt. I would immediately feel guilty over saying such harsh words toward him, but I felt my actions were justified.

"At our next session she handed me a paper plate and a tube of toothpaste. She told me to squeeze every last drop of toothpaste out of the tube. I was confused but did as she asked. She then handed me a plastic knife and asked me to put the toothpaste back inside the tube. After numerous attempts it became obvious that it was impossible. She handed me a piece of paper on which she had written three Scripture verses. The first was James 1:19 about how we must be quick to listen, slow to speak and slow to become angry.[10] Next was Matthew 12:34 about how the mouth speaks what the heart is full of.[12] And the last verse was James 3:8 about humans being incapable of taming the tongue; that it is a restless evil, full of deadly poison.[13]

"She said that it is understandable that I am battling these feelings after such a traumatic event. But she also warned that my tongue was poisoning my marriage and that I needed God's help to tame it. She asked for the piece of paper back and wrote one more verse on it. 'The tongue has the power of life and death...[14]' She warned that I could bring death to my marriage, or possibly worse, if I did not control my words.

"She suggested that every time I brush my teeth to take a moment and remember the exercise she had me do. Just like the toothpaste cannot be put back into the tube, neither can my words return to my mouth. I need to continually pray for God's help. I cannot do it alone.

"At first, I wanted to argue my side; why I deserved to say those things to James. But deep down, I knew she was right. These feelings had such a grip on me and it would only be with God's help that I could possibly break free of them. Before I left, she asked me to try and be quick to listen and not to speak the next time I saw James. I promised her I would try.

"A few days later, James and I met at a park to talk. Before I walked over to him I read the verses on the piece of paper and asked God to please be with me and help me control my tongue. After an awkward greeting we sat down. Normally, I would have started in on my verbal tirade but instead I looked at James, studied him. There were large bags under his blood shot eyes. And there was such pain behind them that I almost had to look away. As my eyes scanned over him I was shocked at how disheveled and frail he was. Even though I didn't feel like it I reached for his hand.

"Immediately he hung his head and began to cry. I just sat there. All the hurtful words I had once wanted to say had disappeared. He kept saying how sorry he was. I gently rubbed his hand. Then, as if a dam had broken free, he began pouring out his feelings. He told me that he traded in his car because he would get physically ill anytime he was near it. He put all of Junior's things in the nursery and closed the door because it had been too painful to see them. He told me that he cries himself to sleep each night, clutching my pillow because he misses me so.

"I felt the heat from my tears as they fell onto my cheeks. I had been blinded by my own pain. Not only was he feeling guilt over what had happened but I had selfishly run off to stay with my sister and left him to deal with the constant reminders of the baby we had lost. His next words jolted me from my thoughts. He told me that every day since Junior's death he has contemplated suicide. I empathized with him. I, too, had moments when I welcomed death. I wanted the pain to stop and to be with Junior. But, what he said next sent shock waves through me. He told me that my words had taken him to such a deep level of pain that if today was the same as all the other times, then today would be his last day on Earth.

"My counselor had been right! Not only were my words destroying my marriage, they were destroying James! I threw my arms around him. Over and over I told him I was sorry and asked him to forgive me. Somehow, amid our weeping, I heard him say he forgave me. Instead of the heat of anger coursing through me I felt a warm presence fill every part of me. I finally understood the power of forgiveness.

"I won't lie to you and say that everything was wonderful after that. Every day a war was waging against us. James was struggling with guilt, and I was desperately trying to control my emotions and my words. Every time I saw a tube of toothpaste I prayed for God to help me tame my tongue. I talked with my counselor about the daily struggles we were still facing. She shared a verse with me. "The thief comes only to steal and kill and destroy; I have come that they may have life and have it to the full.[15]"

"She said that Satan wants to kill and destroy anything that gets in his way. He is doing everything in his power to keep me from coming through this situation with my marriage, and more importantly, my faith intact. She told me that my testimony could impact so many lives for the glory of God and that infuriates Satan.

He is attacking me because he wants me to stumble. He wants me to harbor these feelings. He knows that I can find peace in God, but he tries to trick me into thinking my anger is justified and that I will only have peace when I let my anger come out through my words.

"She also quoted James 1:2-3. 'Consider it pure joy, my brothers and sisters, whenever you face trials of many kinds, because you know that the testing of your faith produces perseverance.[11]' I have clung to these words daily even though there are times when I feel like giving up. You've heard the saying that God doesn't give you more than you can bear? Well, this was definitely more than I could handle. When I mentioned this to my counselor she added something to that saying. She said that God doesn't give us more than we can handle *with Him*. I wasn't going to make it through this alone."

CHAPTER NINETEEN

"I moved back in with James and we slowly began packing up Junior's things. It was one of the hardest things I have ever done. Each item flooded me with memories of my precious little boy. I kept asking God, "Why?" I didn't understand why God would take him from us. Junior was happy, healthy and *very* loved. I wondered what James and I had done wrong that we deserved to lose our child.

"I mentioned this to my counselor. She said that many people who experience a loss like mine have the same questions. It's natural. She anticipated this conversation and had done some research. She found a message that had been given by Lee Strobel[16] shortly after a shooting at a movie theater. Although that tragedy was quite different from mine, she said that Lee's words were for all who have suffered or are suffering in this world.

"She encouraged me to read the entire message myself but shared some key points. Lee gave five points of light to help those who are asking why God allows tragedy and suffering. She shared four of them with me. Lee said that the first point we need to remember is that God did not create evil or suffering. However, Lee clarifies that God *did* create the *potential* for evil to enter the world in order to create the potential for genuine goodness and love. When God created humans, He did not want us to be little robots who automatically love Him. He wanted us to experience real love. So, He gave us free will. We can choose to love or not. Just like we can choose to forgive or withhold forgiveness.

"But with this free will comes great responsibility. Unfortunately, Adam and Eve succumbed to temptation when they ate from the Tree of Knowledge; thus ushering sin into this world.

We all face temptation. We all have choices to make. And we all sin. But we should not be discouraged. Lee's second point is that God can use suffering to accomplish good. The Bible reminds us that, '…in all things God works for the good of those who love Him…[17]'

"My counselor said that it may seem impossible to foresee anything good coming from the death of our son; but nothing is impossible with God.[9] We don't always get the answers we seek this side of Heaven. That is where trust and faith come in.

"There are countless stories in the Bible of suffering. Job had everything taken from him. There was Joseph who was sold into slavery by his brothers. Paul was imprisoned and beaten repeatedly yet praised God through it all. And the greatest story of triumph over tragedy is the story of Jesus. Jesus was betrayed, rejected, tortured and killed. But through His death and resurrection we are given eternal life in Heaven. After all of that, after the immense love God has shown us, why would He not bring good out of our suffering too?

"Another point Lee made is that our suffering pales in comparison to what God has in store for us. In Romans, Paul says, 'For I consider that the sufferings of this present time are not worth comparing with the glory that is to be revealed to us.[18]' This leads into another of Lee's points. We can either decide to turn away from God or run to Him for peace and courage when we face tragedy and suffering. I have heard it said that you can either choose to be bitter or better. The difference is only one letter. I could choose to focus on the 'i'- the *i*mmediate moment, how *I* was wronged and turn *i*nward. Or I could focus on the 'e'- *e*ternity with God, and Junior, and *e*vangelism; how I can use my tragedy to bring others to Jesus.

"As soon as I got home I read the entire message from Lee and began jotting down the verses on post-it notes and placing them throughout the house. It was a way to encourage me, and James, as we continued to heal. After several weeks we finally felt ready to go back to work. Eventually, we fell back into a routine and even discussed trying to have another child. No one could ever replace Junior. We just wanted to experience that love again. After a year of trying it was becoming more and more evident that we might not have another child of our own.

"All those feelings of anger and pain reemerged whenever my period came. I found myself asking God, 'Why?' all over again. We had been sharing our story with others and seeing God work through our testimony. We also talked with the director at Junior's daycare about creating a more accurate attendance system so that parents are called immediately if their child is not dropped off on a designated day. Several months after the system was implemented the director called to tell us that they notified a parent whose daughter was absent, and she was horrified when she realized she had forgotten her in the car. Thankfully, the child was okay. She had not been left in the car for very long.

"Part of me was relieved that the child was safe. Another part of me was angry. If only they had called *me*! Every day I was fighting to get better and not stay bitter. We were doing everything possible to give glory to God through this difficult time. So, why was He denying us another child?

"James had mentioned adoption several times. I guess I was being a bit selfish. Junior had been a part of us and I wanted that again. I didn't think I could love an adopted child the same way. So, I told James that I wanted to keep trying, at least for another year.

"About six months later James was offered a promotion, but it would require us to move. If we moved, we would be moving away from family, from a church we loved and from counselors who have helped us immeasurably. So we started praying about it. Then, one day as I was driving home after an extremely stressful day at the office, I started to wonder if stress was interfering with me getting pregnant. If James took this new job his pay would increase substantially. Then I would have the freedom to find a job that was less stressful since we would not be as dependent on my income anymore.

"That is why we are here. We decided to take a leap of faith and move. James loves his new job and the people he works with. I absolutely adore the animals and the people at the shelter. And working at the shelter has opened my eyes in so many ways. I am more understanding and forgiving because of the inmates, and I have met wonderful people like you.

"I used to think that life was made up of random events, coincidences. I don't believe that anymore. Instead, I believe that God puts events and people in our lives for a reason. It's kind of like a puzzle. These people and events are connected somehow, but we only get to see a few pieces at a time. Only God knows what the big picture will look like. I've written down some songs I would like you to listen to. One of them is *Already There* by Casting Crowns.[19] To God, our future is like a memory. He's already there.

"My faith in God is stronger today than it has ever been, and it is because I leaned on Him during my tragedy. My marriage is stronger because we put our focus on God instead of our loss. And, because of my job at the shelter, I am ready to adopt. Seeing the way those animals long to be loved made me realize that there are children in this world who feel the same way. When we discussed James 1:27[20] during Bible study, I knew in my heart that God was talking to me. We need to look after orphans. I don't know if I ever would have opened my heart to the idea of adopting if it hadn't been for this job, and for *you.*

"I used to call Junior's death a tragedy. After being in God's Word, especially the book of James, I now call it a trial. Our Bible study workbook said that trials are only tragic if they do not accomplish anything in our life.[21] If I stay inward and bitter I cannot honor God, or Junior. When I started going to Bible study with you I thought God had put you in my life to help me. But after hearing your story, my prayer is that somehow my story will help you. "

CHAPTER TWENTY

Mollie sat there, speechless. She hadn't even noticed she had been crying. Ruby's words had cut deep. But instead of feeling pain it was more of a release, like when a doctor cuts into an abscess to relieve the pressure and release the infection. The anger and unforgiveness Mollie was harboring was becoming an infection, a poison. She too thought she was justified in her feelings, her actions. But Brooke had been right...she was a prisoner. And, like Ruby said, she has a choice whether to be bitter or better.

Is God really going to use Brett's death for something good? Mollie looked at Ruby. Tears were streaming down her cheeks. It had taken such courage and strength for Ruby to share her story. Mollie reached out and hugged her. They sat there for several minutes, neither of them saying a word.

Eventually, Ruby pulled back and looked deep into Mollie's eyes. It was as if she was searching...trying to see if her words had helped Mollie.

"Mollie, I will be praying for you. I pray that God will help you through this time and that you will experience His peace."

"Thank you, Ruby. You are a living testimony to the power of faith and forgiveness, and your story has opened my eyes. Please pray for me. I know I need to forgive the man who killed Brett, but I just can't seem to bring myself to do it. I think my biggest obstacle is getting past the fact that he was drunk. I think I would have forgiven him by now if he hadn't been. I don't see it as an accident.

"But, I realize that I am judging him and I'm reminded from our James study that Jesus is the 'only one Lawgiver and Judge...[22]' I guess you aren't the only one who needed to be in this Bible study," Mollie admitted.

Ruby smiled and took her hand, "There are no coincidences, Sugar."

On the drive home, Mollie began recounting the events since Brett's death. Ruby was right. Everything and everyone in Mollie's life had been placed there by God. If it hadn't been for the class field trip she would have never gone to the shelter and found Buster. She would have never met Ruby and realized that they shared such a common bond. If it weren't for a co-worker telling Mollie about this Bible study then she and Ruby would not have found comfort and conviction in God's Word. And Brooke, sweet Brooke, who, out of love, was telling Mollie what she needed to hear.

As soon as Mollie got home she downloaded *Already There*[19] onto her iPod. She grabbed Buster and headed out the door. As they walked she listened to the words. She couldn't hold back the tears. It was as if the song had been written just for her.

Like the lyrics said, she couldn't see where God was leading her or how all her fears and questions would play out in a world she can't control. Control-she remembered something written in their James workbook. That living the Christian life isn't difficult-it's impossible. It can only be accomplished when Jesus lives through us. The only way that can happen is if we relinquish control of our lives.[23]

If God knows the big picture and how all the pieces of my life will fit, then why am I trying to control things? Mollie was trying to do things her way, and her life felt like it was spinning out of control. She listened to the lyrics again...*And all the chaos comes together in Your hands like a masterpiece of Your picture perfect plan.* In *Your* hands...she touched the necklace Brett had made for her. *Jesus died for me. Why have I been doubting Him and His love?*

The next day, Mollie was sitting at her computer after school. She planned on working on lesson plans but, instead, she pulled out the piece of paper Ruby had given her the night before. On it was a list of several songs for Mollie to listen to. One of the titles caught Mollie's attention immediately. *Forgiveness* by Matthew West.[24]

As Mollie listened to the song, the lyrics spoke right to her heart. *The prisoner that it really frees is you.*

Brooke had told Mollie about the peace she felt after forgiving Blake. Mollie remembered the joy in Matthew's eyes and the warmth she felt when he told her that he forgave her. And then there was Ruby's story. Mollie's mind still grappled with the fact that Ruby has forgiven, *and* still loves, James after everything that had happened. But like Ruby said, forgiveness isn't a feeling, it's an action. Mollie still didn't *feel* like forgiving the man who killed Brett but she didn't want to continue feeling this way. She wanted peace. Holding onto all this anger and pain was wearing on her. She needed God to take over and she knew it was finally time to see him.

CHAPTER TWENTY-ONE

Blake was surprised when the guard told him that he had a visitor. Usually his parents or Brooke visited on the weekend. *Why is someone visiting me on a Wednesday?* Suddenly, a sense of alarm ran through him. *Is something wrong? Did something happen to my mom, my dad?* Blake tried to be patient as he walked behind the guard. Finally, they made it to the visitation area. The guard pointed to a table in the far corner. There was a woman sitting there, her back to them.

At first Blake was confused. The woman sitting at the table had blond hair. Brooke was a brunette. *Perhaps she colored her hair?* Blake's heart started racing as he slowly walked toward her...

Mollie's hands were sweating, her heart racing, as she waited in the visitation area. *What am I going to say? What will he say? Can I do this? Maybe I should leave.* She closed her eyes and prayed. She asked God to be with her and to help her control her tongue. Mollie's plan was to tell him she forgave him and leave. She wasn't there to make a new friend. He had Brooke. She just wanted to forgive and forget.

After waiting for what seemed like forever she heard someone approaching. Slowly, Mollie turned her head. She gasped. It couldn't be! Suddenly, the room felt like it was spinning. She needed to get out of there, now! She stood up to leave and felt him gently grab her arm to stop her. Mollie wanted to rip her arm out of his hand and run. Instead, she looked him square in the eyes. All the hurtful things she wanted to say to him flooded her mind. Mollie opened her mouth, ready to give him a piece of her mind. Instantly, she thought of Ruby. "Be quick to listen. [10]" She closed her mouth.

Mollie thought she was going to faint as she listened to his explanation. As soon as he loosened his grasp, she ran toward the door. She frantically wiped away the tears as she drove to the apartment. Once inside, she went to her nightstand and pulled out the police report. There it was, in black and white. *Why hadn't I noticed this before?*

W

Ruby couldn't stop fidgeting. Mollie had texted her the day before, saying she was ready to see the man who took Brett's life; that she was ready to forgive him. Since Monday night, Ruby had been praying that her story would help Mollie; that one day Mollie would be able to forgive, but she never expected it to happen so quickly. When she texted Mollie back and asked her if she was sure she was ready to take this step, Mollie replied that it was now or never.

So, when Mollie texted again that morning and said that today was the day, Ruby immediately started praying for her and for the man Mollie was about to meet. Throughout the day, Ruby continued to feel an intense need to pray for them. She couldn't explain it. She just had this feeling that something was going to happen; that it wasn't going to go according to Mollie's plan.

Lord, please be with Mollie. She is in such a delicate state right now. Only You know what will happen today. She is trying to do the right thing. Please Lord, help her get through this.

Ruby glanced at the clock. She was sure that Mollie would have called or texted her by now. *Why hasn't she called? What happened Lord? Should I call her?*

CHAPTER TWENTY-TWO

Blake fell into a chair as soon as Mollie left. The shock had seemingly worn off and now he was coming to terms with what had just happened. It still didn't seem possible. Of all the people in all the world...

It seemed like a cruel trick. But, it was an innocent mistake. Neither of them had a clue. He tried to explain how it happened, but when she looked at him, there was such pain and hatred behind those beautiful blue eyes. If looks could kill then he would be a dead man.

Blake's heart was breaking and racing all at the same time. She had always been so kind, never judging him or asking why he was an inmate. And, maybe it's crazy, but he thought that there was something between them, a connection. For the past few weeks Blake had secretly dreamed about running into her once his sentence had been served; that somehow she could love him and they would live happily ever after. *Happily ever after?* This wasn't a fairy tale, and he could tell after today that there was absolutely *no* way his dream would ever come true.

And now it was crystal clear that the only connection they have is that night when he took her husband away from her. She said she had recently lost a loved one. *Why didn't she tell me it was her husband? Maybe then I would have put the pieces together. It doesn't matter now. I will probably never see her again.*

He put his head in his hands. *Why Lord? Why her?* It had been hard enough getting through each day knowing that someone was dead because of his action. But to know that he had hurt *her*! Not only did Blake kill her husband, but now he worried that she thinks he tried to trick her; that he had known who she was the whole time.

That was the furthest thing from the truth. When Blake was assigned to the shelter they talked about how it was a clean slate. Other than the orange shirt, no one would know his story. He assumed it was a chance to reinvent himself. They said he could even use a different name if he would like. Blake thought about it for a while and decided to use his middle name, Steven.

Blake's attorney had told him the name of the man he had killed and that the victim's wife had also been in the car, but that she suffered only minor injuries. Minor injuries. There was nothing minor about the pain she was feeling. No one ever told Blake the wife's name. He was sure no one ever told her his *middle* name. Why would they? It wasn't that important a detail.

Why Lord? Why did You have us meet at the shelter? Why are You adding to her pain? You may have forgiven me but she never will. Not after this. Why Lord? I don't understand. Help me understand!

W

Mollie clutched the police report and fell onto her bed. *How could I have been so blind? How could I have let him into my-? No! It was nothing. I feel nothing toward him, nothing but hatred. Did he know all along? He looked just as surprised as I was but it doesn't matter. I am such a fool. Any time I let someone in I get hurt. I am done. I want to be left alone.*

Suddenly, Mollie felt Buster nudging her with his nose. She looked at him. She wanted to hate him too. He had been *his* favorite at the shelter. It sickened her to admit that it was one of the reasons she adopted Buster in the first place. But Mollie could never hate Buster. Every time she looked into his eyes she saw unconditional love. It was as if he could sense when she needed him.

Her whole body ached as she got up off the bed. She wondered if a walk and some fresh air would help. Buster was thankful to be outside, and the walk gave Mollie time to think. *Will St- Blake tell Brooke? Will he tell Ruby? What will they think of me? What will people say?* Mollie knew what to do. She had a plan and her mind was made up. She would pour herself into her teaching and finish out the school year. Then, she would turn in her letter of resignation. She could stay in her apartment until her lease runs out at the end of July and then move back home. She would work out the rest of the details later. For now, all that mattered was getting out of there as soon as she could.

Mollie looked at her phone to see what time it was. That's when she noticed a text message from Ruby. Mollie wanted to tell Ruby what happened but she couldn't. She envisioned Ruby defending him. She would tell Mollie all the wonderful qualities he possesses. How it *had* to have been an accident. Ruby would remind her of her feelings for him.

But Mollie was too ashamed to call her. She felt like a fool. She thought she could read people, but the past few days had proven otherwise. Brooke, who Mollie *thought* was her best friend, had been keeping secrets from her and now this. She had been so naive to think that Steven was a good person who had simply made a minor mistake. He killed Brett, and what hurt the most was that he had been drinking *while* he was driving. At least that is what the police report concluded. *How could he? How could I have been so wrong about him?*

Mollie put her phone back into her pocket. She needed to start distancing herself from Ruby, from Brooke...from everyone. Besides, she would be moving in a few months and would probably never be back here again. Mollie thought that after losing Brett nothing else could ever hurt her, that the agonizing pain she has felt has somehow numbed her to future pain. But she was wrong. Betrayal cuts deep, possibly deeper than loss. She felt so alone. And she felt angry. *Why Lord? I was trying to do the right thing. I wish I had never gone there, that I never knew...*

W

Blake spent the rest of the day in his cell. As hard as he tried, he could not erase the memory of that look in her eyes. It was a mixture of intense pain and hatred that would haunt him for the rest of his life. The one ray of hope that Blake had been clinging to was gone.

He'd met this incredible woman who knew he had a history and it didn't matter. It didn't define him in her eyes. From the moment they met, Blake was sure there was something between them, but maybe he was being *too* hopeful. Because of her, he thought he might actually get a second chance. That maybe, just maybe, God would bless him with love even after what he had done.

Blake wanted to ask God to *make* her forgive him but, he knew that wasn't right. He didn't want someone forced into forgiving him any more than he would want someone forced into loving him. It was her choice. All he could do was pray that God would place people and circumstances in her life that would soften her heart and open it up to the possibility of forgiving him. He had totally given up on the idea of her ever loving him. Forgiveness was already a stretch; love would be an impossibility.

Blake picked up his Bible. He needed God's Word, His assurance. He found the verse he has read almost daily since his sentencing. It was because of Brooke that he even knew of this verse. If only he had mentioned Mollie to Brooke during one of her visits. If he had known, he would have distanced himself from her. He wouldn't have let her into his heart, but it was too late now.

Blake turned to Jeremiah 29:11. "'For I know the plans I have for you,' declares the LORD, 'plans to prosper you and not to harm you, plans to give you hope and a future. [25]'" He used to have such faith in these words, but, after today, he could sense that his faith was wavering. *Really Lord? You have plans for me? To give me hope and a future?* Blake didn't think he could feel any worse than that day of the accident but he was wrong. Brett was in Heaven. He wasn't suffering. Mollie was, and it was all because of him. The weight of that guilt was too much. Blake began to sob and cried himself to sleep.

CHAPTER TWENTY-THREE

Brooke was worried. She had never gone this long without talking to Mollie. She desperately wanted to talk to her; to know that she was okay. And, Brooke wanted to tell her everything. She should have never kept those secrets from Mollie and now she was doing it again. *It doesn't matter what her reaction will be. She needs to know.* But Brooke knew she couldn't tell Mollie over the phone or through a text.

It would be a couple of weeks before Brooke would be visiting her parents again. She hated even waiting one more day to tell Mollie, but she had to do this in person. *A couple of weeks won't change anything. Perhaps, by then, Mollie will understand.* All Brooke could do until then was keep Mollie in her prayers. Brooke sensed that Mollie needed prayer, now more than ever…

W

As Ruby drove to the shelter Thursday morning she couldn't shake the feeling that something was wrong. She had texted Mollie and asked how the meeting went. An uneasy feeling settled into Ruby's stomach when Mollie didn't respond. *What happened, Lord? Is she okay?*

Just as Ruby sat down at her desk, she saw Steven out of the corner of her eye. He was pushing a cart loaded with bags of dog food. There was something different about him today. She studied him as he walked by. Normally, he would say hi and smile. But today…today he shuffled by, his head hanging down   .

"Hey Sugar! What's wrong? You feelin' okay?" she asked.

He looked up at her, and Ruby could tell immediately that he had been crying. And, the light was gone from his eyes. The last time she saw eyes like his was when she looked into James' eyes that day at the park.

"Steven! What is it? What's wrong?" Ruby exclaimed.

Ruby was sure that her mouth was wide open the entire time Steven spoke. She just couldn't believe it! *He was the drunk driver who killed Mollie's husband?* She immediately remembered her flippant remark about how none of the inmates here could have possibly done something as serious as kill someone. *How could I have been so thoughtless? I don't know their backgrounds. Poor Mollie!*

She listened as Steven poured his heart out. She could tell that his remorse was genuine. He never intended to hurt anyone that day of the accident, and he certainly didn't mean to hurt Mollie.

"I contemplated telling the guard that I was too sick to work today, but the idea of sitting in my cell, reliving Mollie's visit, was too much. The one thing I hadn't planned on was the wave of emotions that hit me the moment I walked through these doors. Everywhere I look I am reminded of her."

As he spoke, he confirmed Ruby's suspicions that there was something between him and Mollie. She *knew* they had developed feelings for one another, even though they were afraid to admit it. He said that the time they spent together at the shelter had given him hope; hope for a future that would include love, *real* love. But now that hope was gone. "I don't deserve a future and I certainly don't deserve love," he added as tears streamed down his face.

Ruby had heard these words before. Her husband had struggled with these same thoughts and emotions after Junior's death. She never planned on telling Steven her story, but she could feel God nudging her to do it.

As she told the story about that dreadful day she saw disbelief and sadness in Steven's eyes. He was completely unaware of what she and her husband have been through. Ruby took his hand in hers as she continued, "The truth is, no one knows what someone else has been through or is going through. Most people walk around giving the impression that everything is fine; that life is good. We put up walls to keep others from knowing just how much pain is within us. Pride keeps us from letting others in."

"God opposes the proud, but gives grace to the humble.[26] It has definitely been a process for me, and James, to learn this truth. We were both apprehensive about seeing a counselor. The thoughts and emotions that were consuming us were not something we wanted others to know about. It was only when we humbled ourselves and let others into those darkest parts of our hearts that we began to heal. We thank God every day that we found Christian counselors. With every session, God's Word was poured into us. We found peace and comfort in Scripture. And, we also found guidance and conviction. It felt more natural to harbor our feelings of anger and bitterness than to forgive. But nothing worth working for comes easy. That has been our motto ever since that day at the park. Whenever either of us feels like giving up, we remember that saying and go to God's Word."

Steven didn't speak. He just sat there, astonishment written all over his face. He reached toward Ruby and hugged her hard. She felt his body shake as he sobbed. Everything about the moment reminded her of James, and she knew what needed to be done. Only James could truly understand what Steven is going through.

Ruby knew beyond a shadow of doubt that it was no accident, no coincidence that she was at this place, at this time, and surrounded by these people. It was a Divine Appointment scheduled by God Himself. As they sat there together, Steven holding on for dear life, Ruby thanked God for helping her to be open to moments like this. It would have been so easy not to invest in others. Life gets busy and people tend to put relationships with others toward the bottom of their to-do list. But God is a relational God. He longs for fellowship with us, and we were created to be in fellowship with others.

It is our human nature that wants to turn inward and shut everyone and everything out, especially when life gets hard. We focus on disappointments or hurts that others may have caused, and we start to think that if we keep our distance that we can't get hurt again. We forget all the blessings and fullness we experience because of those around us. The same can be true with our relationship with God. When we are facing a trial it is easier to start questioning God and distance ourselves from Him. How quickly we forget all the good things He has done in our lives. When we keep God and others out we are actually adding to our pain. Jesus experienced a magnitude of pain and suffering, and it wasn't just to give us eternal life with Him. He did it so he could empathize with whatever we may be going through. Who better to turn to than Him?

Ruby pulled back from Steven and looked him in the eyes. "Steven, does the prison have visitation on Fridays?" she asked.

"Yes, they do," he replied with a puzzled look on his face.

"Then my husband, James, will be stopping by tomorrow to see you. I think the two of you need to talk."

"Yes ma'am. I would like that."

"I know that it is going to be an especially difficult day for you so I have an idea. Today you will be in charge of walking all of the dogs. As soon as I see you approaching the shelter I will have Trevor bring up another dog. The two of you can exchange animals and we will continue to do this until your shift is up. How does that sound?" Ruby asked.

"That would be wonderful, Ruby. I just don't think I can put on a happy face around the shelter, at least not today. Maybe by Tuesday I will be doing better. Thank you so much for doing this for me," he said, tears gathering once again in his eyes.

Ruby put her arms around him. "Sugar, that's what friends are for."

Steven walked over to the front doors as Ruby asked Trevor to bring out one of the dogs for a walk. Ruby took a moment to pray for Steven as he walked out the door. *Lord, please help him. He needs You, now more than ever.*

CHAPTER TWENTY-FOUR

The next day, Blake anxiously awaited James' visit. He still couldn't believe what Ruby had told him. He never imagined that she has experienced such pain and loss. *And James? How did he ever get through it? How does he still get through it?*

Blake was still struggling just to function under the suffocating weight of his guilt and yet he could not begin to comprehend what James has gone through. *How can I begin to understand the pain and guilt he must be feeling after the death of his son?*

There was no doubt that Junior's death had been an accident. And Blake was certain that James was forgiven. But for Blake, he still felt unworthy of forgiveness. He had been so selfish, and because of his actions a man is dead and a woman he cares a great deal for is suffering. Most days it was difficult to look in the mirror and face the reality of all that he had done.

Blake was startled when the guard came to his cell and announced that he had a visitor. His heart immediately began racing and so did his mind. He had so many questions to ask James. He prayed that God would speak through James. And that maybe, somehow, he could help James.

James stood as Blake approached the table. He was tall with a kind smile. But if you looked closely, you could see the toll his pain has taken on him. He looked considerably older than his age. Worry lines scattered his forehead. There was a light in his eyes but there was also a darkness buried deep. Blake could see it clearly because he sees it in his own eyes every time he looks in the mirror; a constant reminder of that night.

"Thank you so much for coming to visit me. I really appreciate it," Blake said nervously.

"After Ruby shared your story with me I knew, just like she did, that I needed to come," he said kindly. "God continues to show me how He can use our story to help others. And even though it is painful to talk about that day, it also seems to help. When I look back at the events that have happened since Junior's death I can, without a doubt, see God's hand in all of it. So, even though there is pain in remembering, there is also peace."

"I guess that is where I am struggling. I feel like I am right in the middle of it and I can't see God working in my life, at least not yet," Blake replied.

"I felt that way once too. And I felt unworthy of forgiveness. Even though Junior's death was an accident I couldn't release the grip that guilt had on me. Every day was a struggle just to breathe, to function. Many days I contemplated suicide. I couldn't see beyond the moment, beyond the pain. But we are not supposed to know the future. Only God does. My counselor gave me a list of songs to listen to. I have written them down for you. Two songs that really helped me through those dark days were *Worn*[27] and *By Your Side*[28] by Tenth Avenue North."

James pulled out an iPod and began playing them, one after the other. The lyrics spoke to the very depths of Blake's soul. He felt the tears well up inside him. He tried forcing them back, but it was impossible.

"Even though I believed that God was by my side, it was as if my mind needed something to fixate on, and its target became Ruby. I was consumed with worry and doubt as to whether she would ever forgive me or still love me. I felt incomplete without her, especially with Junior gone. I didn't want to live without her. At Junior's visitation she told me she forgave me, and I was elated. But then her emotions would grab a hold of her, and she would attack me with her words. I knew her feelings were justified and that my actions had caused them. I was constantly on an emotional rollercoaster and felt like I was going to crash.

"I talked to my counselor about it. He told me that we tend to look for happiness and fulfillment through others. But, unfortunately, we are all human and will inevitably let each other down. True peace and love can only come from God. He never changes. He will never let us down. He will never stop loving us. He will never withhold forgiveness when we repent. Like that second song says, 'Why am I looking for love as if God is not enough?'

"The only way I was ever going to start healing and move forward was if I came to terms with the fact that Ruby might never forgive me. That she may no longer love me. I couldn't base my happiness on her. It had to be in Christ and Christ alone. Yet, I would still cry myself to sleep each night, longing for her.

"All I could do was pray and rest in the knowledge that God had forgiven me and loves me. Whenever I prayed for Ruby I started by saying, 'If it is Your will Lord, please help her forgive me and love me again.' I left it in God's hands. As much as I struggled with the thought that she might never love me or forgive me I had to realize that whatever happened, God was in control.

"That is my advice to you in regards to Mollie. Ruby told me that there may be a connection between you two that goes beyond the accident. Only God knows if she will ever forgive you or one day even love you. It may seem impossible right now, and please know I am not making any predictions, but I can tell you that there is one truth I have witnessed time and time again; *nothing* is impossible with God.[9]"

Blake knew that James' words were exactly what he needed to hear. Ever since Mollie's visit, Blake began telling himself that if she was somehow able to forgive him, then everything would be better; that he would finally feel happiness again. Blake was putting "all of his eggs into one basket" and it was clear that it was the wrong basket. As much as the thought broke his heart, he had to come to terms with the fact that she may never forgive him.

His happiness cannot revolve around another person; it can only come from God. The sooner he could get his heart to understand this, the sooner he could heal and move forward. Blake knew what he needed to do. He needed to pray. He needed to pray for Mollie and he needed to pray for himself.

"Blake," James continued, "I know we have only just met, but I was wondering if I could ask you a personal question."

"Of course."

"Blake, have you asked Jesus into your heart?"

James' question caught Blake off-guard. "I...I don't know. I don't think so," he replied.

"When I was a child, I saw a painting of Jesus standing at a door. As I studied the picture, I noticed that the handle on the outside of the door was missing. I immediately told my dad that the painter had forgotten about the door knob. My father smiled and said, 'No son. It wasn't forgotten. There is meaning in that painting. You see, the only way Jesus may enter is if He is let in.' In the Bible, Jesus says, 'Behold, I stand at the door and knock. If anyone hears My voice and opens the door, I will come in to him and eat with him, and he with Me. [29]' In Romans it says that, 'If you confess with your mouth that Jesus is Lord and believe in your heart that God raised Him from the dead, then you will be saved. [30]' By confessing that Jesus is Lord and asking Him into our hearts, we become God's children and will spend eternity in Heaven with Him. Blake, I have something for you," James said as he reached into his pocket and pulled out a small piece of paper.

"I want you to have this for when you are ready," James continued as he handed it to Blake.

Blake carefully opened the paper and read the title. "I'm ready," Blake said as he stared at the paper. "I don't want to wait another minute."

Blake steadied his hands as he began to read the words. "The Sinner's Prayer: Heavenly Father, have mercy on me, a sinner. I believe in You and that Your Word is true. I believe that Jesus Christ is the Son of the living God and that He died on the cross so that I may now have forgiveness for my sins and eternal life. I know that without You in my heart my life is meaningless.

99

"I believe in my heart that You, Lord God, raised Him from the dead. Please Jesus forgive me, for every sin I have ever committed or done in my heart, please Lord Jesus forgive me and come into my heart as my personal Lord and Savior today. I need You to be my Father and my friend.

"I give you my life and ask You to take full control from this moment on; I pray this in the name of Jesus Christ. Amen.[31]"

Blake closed his eyes and clutched the paper as tears streamed down his face. He felt a hand upon his and opened his eyes.

"Welcome to the family, brother," James said with a smile as tears welled up in his eyes.

James offered to come by once a week and even suggested that they do a Bible study together. Blake was speechless. James had only known him for an hour and was already planning ways for them to stay connected, to each other and to God's Word. *Lord, may You use me the way You are using James. I am in awe of his faith and compassion, and I know that it all comes from You. Thank You for putting him, and Ruby, in my life.*

CHAPTER TWENTY-FIVE

Days turned into weeks and Mollie's plan seemed to be working beautifully. She was devoting more time to her work, and her students were thriving. Mollie even found herself laughing along with her students at times. She also started running more with Buster and really felt like she had found her stride, in running and in life.

She was still getting calls and texts from Ruby and Brooke but they would stop eventually. It was only a matter of time before they would give up and move on. Mollie seemed to have found peace, at least during the day. At night was a different story. She would lie awake, her mind replaying memories of Brett, the crash, Steven/Blake. All of it would start swirling around in her head and made it difficult to sleep.

When Mollie called her parents and told them about her plan to move back home she could hear the excitement in their voices. But when she mentioned that she had not talked to Brooke in quite some time, their voices were filled with concern.

"Honey, what's going on? Why haven't you spoken to Brooke?" her mom asked.

Mollie began telling Karen about Brooke visiting Blake and the pregnancy. "I just can't understand how she could keep those things from me. She said she was worried about how I would react. There's no doubt I would have been shocked, and perhaps angry, but at least I wouldn't have felt betrayed too."

"When I confided in my friend Ruby she shared her heartbreaking story about her son's death. He was only a few months old and died from heatstroke when Ruby's husband, James, accidentally left him in the car instead of taking him to daycare. She not only forgave James; she *loves* him, and they are still married today. After hearing her story, being forgiven by Matthew, and Brooke telling me about the peace she has felt ever since forgiving Blake I thought I was ready to forgive.

"I was until I realized that Blake is Steven."

"Wait a minute! You shared so much, and I want to talk more about Ruby and her story, but what did you say? Steven, from the shelter, is Blake?" Mollie could hear the disbelief in her mother's voice.

"He used his middle name. I didn't believe it until I got home and looked at the police report. There it was in black and white...Blake *Steven* Williams. I had been so blind. I thought he was a nice guy; that maybe he had taken some money from his employer or...it doesn't matter. I just didn't think he had done something so..." Mollie stopped, unable to finish.

She could tell that her mom wanted to say something. She probably wanted to tell Mollie the same thing Brooke said. Humans are the ones who rank sin. God doesn't. And Jesus didn't die for *some* sins, He died for *all* sin.

But Karen could tell that Mollie wasn't in the mood to hear it, not again, not now. And Mollie sensed Karen's uneasiness about her spending so much time alone. Deep down Mollie knew that she wasn't just distancing herself from those around her; she was distancing herself from God. She *knew* it wasn't right. She *knew* she should be running to God, not from Him. But she just didn't *feel* like it.

The rest of the school year flew by quickly, and suddenly it was the students' last day. A gamut of emotions was taking place within Mollie. She was sad to see their time together end. Because of these little ones, Mollie had been able to take her focus off of her pain and see the simple joys in life. She was delighted to see how far they had come since their first day together. They had grown in so many ways.   And Mollie was anxious...anxious to turn in her letter of resignation.

She thought about turning it in that day, but the teachers still had two work days to get rooms packed up and paperwork finished, and she didn't want to be bombarded with questions. She would use these work days to pack up her room and tie up loose ends and *then* turn in her resignation. Other than her parents, she hadn't told anyone about her plans. Mollie knew that her principal would be shocked, as well as the rest of the staff. She was probably taking the coward's approach, but she just couldn't submit herself to all their questions and concerned looks.

Thankfully, over the next two days all of the other teachers were so busy that no one stopped by Mollie's room to discover that she was packing everything up. By the end of the second day the walls were bare. All that was left was a mound of boxes in the middle of the room. After putting the last of the boxes in her car, Mollie walked down the hallway to Mrs. Higgins' office. She noticed that almost all of the teachers were gone. Her heart began racing and her stomach was twisting and turning into a million knots. It was time.

She walked up to Mrs. Higgins' office and gently knocked on the door. As Mollie stepped in, Mrs. Higgins looked up from her desk.

"Hi Mollie. Come in," she said as she sat back in her chair.

"Hi Mrs. Higgins," Mollie replied as she sat down.

"Ready to check out for the summer?" she asked smiling.

"Actually, I am here to give you my letter of resignation," Mollie said, unable to look her in the eyes.

"Oh! Is everything okay?"

"Ever since Brett's death, things have been hard. Everywhere I look I am reminded of him. I plan to move back home and maybe get a teaching job or just do some subbing. I'm still not sure. I just feel like I need a change," she said, tears gathering in the corners of her eyes.

"I understand. We will miss you terribly, and if you ever find yourself back here and looking for a teaching job please give me a call. I would love to have you back," Mrs. Higgins replied, her eyes glistening.

"Thank you," Mollie managed to say as the tears began falling down her cheeks.

Mrs. Higgins stood up and came around her desk to give Mollie a hug. For the first time, Mollie began to question her plans. *Why am I leaving a school I love? Mrs. Higgins and the staff are absolutely amazing. But what if they found out that I had developed feelings for the man who killed Brett? What would they think of me? What would they say? No, it's for the best. I have to get out of here.*

Over the next few days there were moments when Mollie thought about moving back home before the end of July. But she liked the idea of having some time all to herself. Although Karen would be delicate, Mollie knew her mom would have lots of questions, and she just wasn't ready to answer them, not yet.

Mollie had feared that once school was out that the days would drag on but, instead, she was surprised at how quickly time was passing. She and Buster would go for walks in the mornings and out for a run at night. The rest of the time she filled with reading, painting, or watching movies; anything to take her mind off of Brett and the others.

She was deeply lost in a book when she heard her phone ring. Mollie looked at it expecting to see Brooke or Ruby's name appear. Instead, it was Derek. *Is something wrong, or is Brooke trying to trick me into answering? I guess I'll find out.*

"Hello," she answered.

"Mollie, it's Derek. Can you talk?" he asked, and she could hear the nervousness in his voice.

"Yes," Mollie replied, matter-of-factly.

"Mollie, there is something we need to tell you. As you know, Brooke has been visiting Blake for some time and has seen such a change in him; a change that can only come from God. We have been praying over this for months and have decided to write letters to the judge asking that Blake's sentence be reduced and that he be set free," he said, his voice trembling.

Mollie had to sit down. As the shock wore off her anger grew. "And you expect me to write a letter too?" she snapped.

"Not at all. We just wanted you to know. We understand if you are not ready…"

"I'll *never* be ready!" she interrupted. "Obviously, it is *your* choice to do this. I will not stand in your way," Mollie said as she felt heat penetrating every part of her.

"Mollie…"

"I have to go Derek. Good-bye," she said and hung up. She didn't want to hear any more. He had said enough already. His words ran through Mollie's mind. *They are going to try to get Blake released? After what he did? How is serving a few months in prison honoring Brett's life? Why am I feeling like the bad guy? Just another reason to get out of here.*

After Derek's call Mollie decided to get a different phone number. Then the calls and texts from Ruby, Brooke, teachers…everyone would finally stop. Her parents and siblings would be the only people who would know her new number, and Mollie would make sure they promised to keep it that way.

CHAPTER TWENTY-SIX

As the weeks went by, Blake continued to feel a change taking place inside him. James' testimony and the Bible study were speaking directly to him. He was finally feeling the hand of God working in his life. And for the first time in a long time, Blake felt strong enough to make it through his prison sentence and have hope for a future beyond those walls. He knew it was because he was relying on Jesus. No one else could get him through this.

Yet, just like James warned, Blake's mind would wander to thoughts of Mollie, and he would become consumed with a desire for her forgiveness, for her. There were still moments when he would question God. *Why? Why did it have to be her? Why couldn't she have been some random stranger, like I thought she was. And why did I develop feelings so quickly for her? I barely know her.*

Blake shook his head, trying to clear his mind, but it was no use. *Why did she visit the prison in the first place? Was she going to forgive me? Has she changed her mind?* Blake wished he could ask Brooke, but she had not visited him since Mollie's visit. He began to worry that somehow Brooke had changed her mind too; that she no longer forgave him. Blake's thoughts were interrupted by the sound of a guard's voice.

"Williams, warden wants to see you," he ordered.

"Yes, sir," Blake replied and immediately started following him.

The guard led Blake to the warden's office and told him to sit down.

Blake's palms began to sweat, and he felt his entire body begin to shake as he waited. *Why is the warden asking to see me? Did I do something wrong?*

He looked up to see the warden enter the room.

"Good afternoon, Mr. Williams. I bet you are wondering why I called you into my office. Well, I won't keep you waiting. You are to appear in court on Monday at nine o'clock," he stated.

"Sir?" Blake asked, confused.

"That is all I have been told. Please make sure that you are clean, dressed and ready to go by eight thirty Monday morning," he replied.

"Yes sir," Blake answered.

As he walked back to his cell, questions flooded Blake's mind. *Do they think my sentence is too short? Are they going to try and add more years? Brooke must have changed her mind. Perhaps she and Mollie have talked the rest of Brett's family into appealing my sentence. Lord, please help me get through the next few days. This not knowing is killing me!*

W

Monday finally arrived and Blake was ready. He had spent the weekend doing extra work around the prison, anything to keep his mind off of this court appearance. He arrived at the courthouse with only a few minutes to spare. Any hope of talking to his attorney beforehand was gone.

As soon as Blake sat down the judge entered the courtroom. Once they were seated again the judge spoke.

"Mr. Williams, we are here today to discuss your sentencing. I want to start by saying that I take crimes that result in death very seriously. So when I received letters from the victim's family asking for your sentence to be reduced and for you to be set free I was going to dismiss them immediately. Only serving four months for taking a life does not seem like justice to me."

Blake sat there, completely stunned. *They wrote letters on my behalf? They want me set free?* Tears began to stream down his face. Even if the judge denied their request, the knowledge of their complete and utter forgiveness would forever be stored in his heart.

"After reading the letters and reviewing a report about the current crowding at the prison I have reached my decision. Mr. Williams, I am granting their request for early release. However, there are some conditions that go along with it. You will be on probation for two years, and during those two years you will visit schools, churches, organizations and such, sharing your story. Hopefully this will keep the events of that day fresh in your memory and keep you from ever repeating it. And my hope is that your testimony will help prevent others from making the same mistake. Mr. Williams, you are a free man. I hope to never see your name come across my desk again."

Blake's legs were so weak that he was almost unable to stand as the judge left the courtroom. Blake turned around, expecting to see Brett's family, but the seats were all empty. Suddenly, he felt someone shaking his hand. It was his attorney and he had a huge smile on his face.

"Congratulations Blake! I need to take care of some paperwork. The bailiff can direct you to a phone to call your parents. They will be thrilled to hear the news! You could have them bring a change of clothes and some shoes. And you will want to begin preparing for these speaking engagements. The judge wants me to start scheduling them the middle of next month. That is only three weeks away. Blake, today is truly a miracle. Judge Stevens *never* grants an early release. Makes ya wonder what those letters said, huh?" he asked with a nudge and then headed toward the door.

As long as Blake lives he will never forget the sound of his mother's wails of joy when he told her the news. And he could hear the emotion in his father's voice as they spoke. Blake couldn't wait for them to get there.

CHAPTER TWENTY-SEVEN

Ever since James' first visit to the prison, Ruby could see a transformation taking place in Steven. And she saw a change in James too. It was just another example of God's perfect plan in action. These two men needed each other. James' advice and guidance was helping Steven get through the moments of guilt and uncertainty. And, by helping Steven, James was in the Word, and he felt a sense of purpose in his life that he had never felt before. There was new life in both of them and it filled Ruby's heart with joy.

But at the same time, she was troubled. She worried about Mollie. It had been well over a month since Mollie visited Steven at the prison, and Ruby had not heard from her. Mollie had not returned any of her calls or texts. Ruby even tried calling from the shelter so Mollie wouldn't recognize the number. Still no answer. And just recently, when Ruby tried calling her, the call would not go through. *Did she change her phone number?* Mollie had stopped going to Bible study too. *Lord, I am worried about her. I fear she is turning from You and from those around her who love her. Please help me reach her. She needs You!*

Ruby thought about looking up Mollie's address from Buster's adoption paperwork. But she could be reprimanded or possibly lose her job if anyone found out. Instead, she would put her trust in God and let Him take care of the details. *Lord, Mollie needs to feel You, to know You are near and that You are with her. Please Lord, show her.*

W

As much as Ruby enjoyed spending time with James on the weekend, she would still wait in anticipation for Monday to come. Weekends were more relaxing, but they also gave her time to think…about Junior. It was a daily battle to fight her feelings of hurt, anger, bitterness and guilt. The shelter was not only a refuge for lost and unwanted animals; it had become her refuge too.

Mondays tend to be quite busy at the shelter, and Ruby was buried in paperwork from the moment she arrived. Several animals had been dropped off over the weekend and were in the process of being examined and observed. Ruby was typing away when she heard the front door open. When she looked up her mouth dropped open in utter disbelief.

There before her was Steven. There were no guards with him, no orange shirt. Ruby tried to speak but nothing came out. There she sat with her mouth, and her eyes, wide open.

"Hello Ruby," he said with a smile.

"What? How? Why?" she stammered.

He walked up to her desk and took her hand in his. "I've been set free Ruby. First by Jesus and now by Brett's family."

Ruby sat there, still unable to speak.

"I had to appear in court today. I thought that maybe they were changing their mind about my sentence; that it needed to be longer. Instead, the judge said that Brett's family wrote letters on my behalf, asking for my sentence to be reduced and for me to be set free. It's a miracle, Ruby! My lawyer even said so. He said that this judge *never* reduces sentences," he said, tears quietly falling.

Ruby jumped up and hugged him. "Praise Jesus! It's a miracle!" she exclaimed.

She pulled back and looked into his eyes, "Mollie?"

"I don't know if she wrote a letter too. The judge did not specify which family members had written to him. And none of Brett's family was in the courtroom today so I wasn't able to talk to them, to thank them. I can't explain it, but I have this feeling that she did not write a letter, that she hasn't forgiven me."

"Well, Sugar, then we'll just keep talking to God about it. And you just *have* to come over for dinner tonight. James will be overjoyed when he hears the news!"

"May I take a rain check? My parents are waiting outside to take me back to their house. I think I should spend my first night with them."

"Of course Sugar! Should I tell James or would you like to surprise him like you did me?" she chuckled.

"It would be fun to surprise him. The look on your face was priceless! Would tomorrow night work to have dinner together?"

"Absolutely! Tomorrow it is! Where are you staying?"

"I plan to stay with my parents for a while. As part of my early release I must visit churches, schools and organizations to share my story. The judge doesn't want me to forget about that awful night. The truth is, I will never forget. And the judge hopes that my story will keep others from making the same mistake. That is my hope and prayer. I don't want anyone to go through this."

"Sounds like you will need a job with some flexibility? Want me to see if we have any openings here?" Ruby asked.

"Oh Ruby! That would be wonderful!"

"Let me work my magic. Why don't you meet me here tomorrow at six o'clock, and you can ride home with me?"

"Perfect! See you tomorrow," he said as he wrapped his arms around her.

"Oh Steven, this is such an answer to prayer!" Ruby whispered as they stood there together.

"Yes it is, Ruby. And please, call me Blake."

"You got it, Sugar. See you tomorrow," she said as Blake left.

Ruby fell into her chair, astounded by what had just happened. She didn't think anything could surprise her; not after what she has been through. There was no denying that it was a miracle that she and James were still together, their marriage and faith intact. And it's a miracle that Blake turned to God during his darkest moments. But this...this was something Ruby had never expected. Then again, we aren't meant to know God's plans, only that His plans are perfect. He had definitely proven that today!

CHAPTER TWENTY-EIGHT

The past few weeks had been peaceful. The only calls or texts Mollie received were from her mother. She could sense the concern in Karen's voice whenever she called.

"Honey, are you sure you don't want to move home now?"

"Mom, it's okay. I am actually enjoying this time to myself. Besides, I only have a few weeks left on my lease. I'll be home before you know it."

"Okay. Have you talked to Brooke or Ruby lately?" Karen asked hesitantly.

"No." Mollie's response was cold and curt.

Karen could sense that this topic was not open for discussion. There were so many questions she wanted to ask and things she wanted to tell her daughter, but she knew that Mollie was not quite ready for it. All she could do was pray for her.

Mollie could tell that she was in a sour mood after talking with her mother. She needed to run, to clear her mind and get her blood pumping. Earlier that day, Mollie noticed Buster limping after their morning walk. After looking carefully at his paw she discovered a piece of glass imbedded into the pad of his foot. Mollie gently removed the glass, cleaned his paw and put some gauze around his foot. She would have to do her evening run alone tonight.

She could see the sadness in Buster's eyes as she got ready for her run. *And some people think dogs don't have feelings? They need to meet Buster.*

Mollie decided to take a different route and run past the baseball stadium. The path would be well lit and safe. She was slowly working herself into her stride when she turned on her iPod.

She thought she picked her "Run" set of songs, but the song that began to play was not familiar. Mollie started listening to the words.

So your life feels like it don't make sense. And you think to yourself, "I'm a good person." So why do these things keep happening? Why you gotta deal with them? You may be knocked down now. But don't forget what He said, He said: "I won't give you more, more than you can take. And I might let you bend, but I won't let you break. And No-o-o-o-o, I'll never ever let you go-o-o-o-o-o." Don't you forget what He said.

Who you are ain't what you're going through. So don't let it get the best of you. 'Cause God knows everything you need. So you ain't gotta worry. You may be knocked down now. But just believe what He said, He said: "I won't give you more, more than you can take. And I might let you bend, but I won't let you break. And No-o-o-o-o, I'll never ever let you go-o-o-o-o-o." Don't you forget what He said.

Don't fear when you go through the fire. Hang on when it's down to the wire. Stand tall and remember what He said: "I won't give you more, more than you can take. And I might let you bend, but I won't let you break...[32]"

Mollie had been so focused on the song that she didn't notice where she was or that she had started crying. *Where did this song come from?* She glanced down at her iPod when, suddenly, shots rang out. Mollie looked up and fell to her knees.

CHAPTER TWENTY-NINE

Brooke wasn't sure how she had gotten through the past few weeks. She had summoned the strength to call Mollie after Derek had told her about the letters and was devastated when she discovered that Mollie had changed her phone number. *I should have been the one to tell her about the letters, to tell her about... And now she has changed her number! Lord, does she hate me that much?*

Fits of crying had become almost as common as breathing for Brooke these past few weeks. Ever since that day at the hospital she has been a wreck. She should have told Mollie about the letters in person, like she planned. But she was such an emotional mess that she asked Derek to call Mollie instead. Brooke prayed that Mollie would answer when she saw Derek's number come up on her phone.

Brooke's prayer was answered, but Derek was so surprised that Mollie *did* answer that he jumped right in to talking about the letters and forgot to tell her the reason *why* first. Brooke hoped that their news would soften Mollie's heart and she would understand. But, by the time Derek remembered, Mollie had already hung up. Now Brooke had no way to tell her.

She was sure that Mollie's parents knew her new number but have been asked not to share it with anyone, including her. *Maybe I should call her parents and tell them about the baby. Maybe they could get the message to Mollie.* Brooke decided to wait until the morning to call Mollie's parents. She didn't have the strength to get through that conversation, not tonight...

W

Mollie managed to look up again. The sky was aglow with every color of the rainbow. She was by the baseball stadium and had completely forgotten that on Friday nights they put on a fireworks display for their fans once the game is over. She was instantly reminded of Brett's proposal on the Fourth of July and the fireworks show she had surprised him with at the conclusion of their wedding reception. Mollie buried her head in her hands and wept. *This is too much Lord. I can't take it anymore. This is too much.* She was about to try and stand up when she realized music was playing.

When I'm feeling all alone, with so far to go. The signs are nowhere on this road, guiding me home. When the night is closing in, it's falling on my skin. Oh God will You come close?

Light, light, light up the sky. You light up the sky to show me You are with me. I, I, I can't deny. No, I can't deny that You are right here with me. You've opened my eyes so I can see You all around me. Light, light, light up the sky. You light up the sky to show me that You are with me.

When the stars are hiding in the clouds I don't feel them shining. When I can't see You beyond my doubt, the silver lining. When I've almost reached the end, like a flood You're rushing in. Your love is rushing in.

Light, light, light up the sky. You light up the sky to show me You are with me. I, I, I can't deny. No, I can't deny that You are right here with me. You've opened my eyes so I can see You all around me. Light, light, light up the sky. You light up the sky to show me that You are with me.

So I run, straight into Your arms. You're the bright and morning sun. To show Your love there's nothing You won't do.

Light, light, light up the sky. You light up the sky to show me You are with me. I, I, I can't deny. No, I can't deny that You are right here with me. You've opened my eyes so I can see You all around me. Light, light, light up the sky. You light up the sky to show me that You are with me.[33]

Mollie was stunned. *Where did this song come from?* She wiped the tears from her eyes and looked at her iPod. Instead of her "Run" folder, she had selected a folder labeled "Ruby." Mollie had completely forgotten that she downloaded all of the songs Ruby had written down for her the night she shared her story about Junior. Ruby had listed so many songs that Mollie didn't have a chance to listen to them all. So, she put them in a folder with Ruby's name on it. It was no coincidence that *this* song played right as Mollie was watching fireworks go off above her. God was at the center of it all...letting her know that He was there, that He had never left her. *But why did Ruby have this song on her list?* She would have to find that out later. Right now she needed to get home.

Mollie stood up, expecting to feel weak. Instead, she felt a renewed sense of strength and purpose course within her. She immediately started running. As she ran home, Mandisa's *Overcomer*[34] blasted through her iPod. Mollie had heard the song numerous times before, but tonight it became her anthem. She *will* overcome with the help of God and her friends and family. But first, she needed to mend some fences, and she knew exactly where to start.

By the time Mollie reached the apartment she felt like she was walking on air, as if a weight had been lifted off her shoulders. Buster was so excited when Mollie asked him if he wanted to go for a ride that she couldn't help but laugh. She dropped to her knees and Buster proceeded to knock her over and cover her in kisses. Not only was God with Mollie, but He had given her Buster to show her what unconditional, uninhibited love is.

In no time Mollie and Buster were at her in-laws' house. Even with a sore paw, Buster was tugging on the leash, begging Mollie to walk faster. She rang the doorbell and realized that her whole body was shaking. She wasn't sure if it was nerves or adrenalin but she didn't have much time to think about it because the door opened immediately.

As soon as Mollie saw who was on the other side she froze. It was Derek. It hadn't crossed her mind that he and Brooke would be visiting. But it wasn't the fact that he was there that startled her. It was how he looked. There were large dark circles under his lifeless eyes. Mollie could always count on Derek's quick, genuine smile but not tonight. It was as if it took all his strength just to stand. Even with his strong, muscular frame he looked frail.

"Derek, is everything okay?" Mollie asked, trying to mask her alarm.

He stepped forward and threw his arms around her and began to sob.

"Derek. What is it? What's wrong? Is it Brooke? The baby?"

He pulled back and collected himself. "Brooke is in the living room."

Mollie followed him inside, Buster close to her side. As soon as they rounded the corner Buster sprinted for the couch and leapt onto Brooke's lap. Mollie was about to scold him and tell him to get down when she saw Brooke wrap her arms around him and bury her face in his fur. Her whole body shook as she wept.

CHAPTER THIRTY

Amid her confusion, Mollie walked over to the couch and sat down. She wanted to ask questions, to get some answers, but the verse from James was echoing in her mind, "Be quick to listen, slow to speak.[10]" She put her hand on Brooke's knee and waited. Mollie turned toward Derek. Tears were quietly streaming down his face as he watched his wife crumble before him. He must have sensed the need to speak, that Brooke was incapable of telling Mollie what was wrong.

"A few weeks ago," he began, trying to steady his voice and his emotions, "we went to the hospital to have the twenty-week ultrasound done. We couldn't wait to see our little one. I was glued to the monitor. Brooke, however, was watching both the monitor and the technician. Maybe it is her medical background, or maybe a mother's intuition, but she knew something wasn't right.

"At first, she didn't tell me about her suspicions and tried to push them out of her mind. It wasn't until the next day, when we got a call from the doctor asking us to come in, that she shared her fears. I assured her that everything was fine. But, I was also concerned as to why the doctor wanted to see us. I wanted to be strong for Brooke. It wasn't until the doctor told us that I lost it.

"Our little girl has Limb-body Wall Complex which means her internal abdominal organs have developed outside her body. We have met with several specialists since the initial diagnosis and the prognosis has never changed...if our baby makes it through delivery she will only live for a short time, perhaps only a couple of hours. The doctors told Brooke that she could choose to terminate the pregnancy or see it through. There was no doubt in her mind; she

119

would carry this precious life, no matter what happens. I have never been more proud of her," he said as he wiped the tears from his eyes.

Mollie sat there, unable to speak, to move. There was so much for her mind, and her heart, to process. She was overwhelmed by grief for Brooke and Derek. And she could also sense the heat of anger welling up within her. *How could You let this happen? First, she loses her only brother and now she will lose her only child, a daughter? She has been the one to show grace and forgiveness to Brett's killer and this is how You repay her? Why?* It took every ounce of self-restraint for Mollie not to show her anger. Instead, she held her dear friend as she sobbed. As much as Mollie wanted to understand what Brooke was going through she couldn't. But she knew someone who could.

Mollie promised to return the next day. It wasn't until she got into the car to leave that she let her anger surface. She yelled at the sky as she drove home. Memories of Ruby's story and the message from Lee Strobel[16] flooded her mind. *God does not create evil or suffering. Instead, He can turn suffering into good. Really? How could any good come from this?* Mollie had already been struggling with that concept as she continued to grieve over Brett's death but now this? *How much more can we take?* The words of Ruby's counselor emerged, "God doesn't give us more than we can handle *with Him.*" There was no way any of them would get through this without God. Mollie wanted to be angry and turn from God but she had already tried that and it had left her feeling more alone and empty than ever before. The only times Mollie felt peace were when she was closest to God.

After a restless night's sleep, Mollie quickly got ready and drove to the animal shelter. She had to see Ruby. She needed to apologize, and she needed Ruby's help. As Mollie sat in her car, nervously waiting for the shelter's doors to be unlocked, she prayed that God would use Ruby to help Brooke. And she prayed that Ruby would be able to forgive her for pushing her away when Mollie needed her the most.

As soon as Mollie saw Ruby unlock the doors she looked down, feeling ashamed. She unhooked her seat belt and was about to open her door when suddenly it flung open. She looked up to see Ruby standing in front of her.

"Oh Sugar! It is so good to see you! I have been thinking about you and praying for you!" she exclaimed wrapping her arms around Mollie. Ruby's excitement and the warmth of her embrace brought Mollie to tears. *How could I have ever doubted her friendship, her love? She isn't judging me.*

"Sugar, what is it? What's wrong?"

They walked into the shelter and went into the conference room for some privacy. Mollie told Ruby about Brooke's unborn child. Tears quietly slid down Ruby's cheeks as she listened. Mollie also told Ruby that she was instantly angry with God when she heard the news. But then, on the drive home, she remembered Ruby's words, her story, and that is what helped her stay focused on getting better and not slipping into bitterness again.

"I know this is a lot to ask, but is there any chance you could visit Brooke? As much as I want to be there for her I think she needs to talk with someone who has experienced a loss like this. I completely understand if this is asking too much."

Ruby took a hold of Mollie's hands. "This is my way of helping God use our story for His glory. And, I know how important it is to not feel alone in our suffering. I think back to when James and I were at our lowest. To this day, I wonder if it would have helped us recover faster if we had joined a support group for parents who have lost young children. Perhaps I would have found the verse in 2 Corinthians sooner that says, 'God comforts us in all our troubles so that we can comfort others.[35]' That verse has become my mission statement. How about you talk to Brooke about it and let me know when and where, and I'll be there?"

"Thank you Ruby! I will!"

Blake had to take a double take when he walked past the front windows. *Could that really be her car? Is she here to see me?* Blake searched every hallway along the kennels and the cages. There was no sign of her. *Perhaps that isn't her car. Or, that is her car, but she is obviously not here to see me.* He fought back the tears that were creeping up. He shook his head and walked to the room with the animals' food. He needed to get to work and get her off his mind.

After the animals were fed, Blake grabbed a leash and let Sam out of his kennel for a walk. As he made his way to the front door he stopped dead in his tracks. *Is that...her perfume?* Blake took a deep breath in. *It is! She must be here!* He peered over the partitions but didn't see her anywhere. He wanted to go back to the kennels to look for her, but Sam was already tugging on the leash, anxious to get outside. As hard as it was to leave, Blake went out the front doors. That was when he saw that her car was gone. *She didn't come to see me. What a fool I am!* Blake took Sam on an extra long walk that day. He needed some time for his emotions to have their way with him before he was ready to go back in.

CHAPTER THIRTY-ONE

Mollie drove straight home after her talk with Ruby. Buster needed his morning walk, and they needed to get to Brooke. Mollie reached for Buster's leash and noticed something fall onto the floor. She looked down and discovered it was the Scripture journal her mother had made for her. She sat down and gazed at the cover.

Mollie gently ran her fingers over the picture of the tree-lined path. *Thy word is a lamp unto my feet, and a light unto my path.*[4] She studied the picture. She had always considered the trees to symbolize God's protection over her, shielding her from harm. But now, as she quietly contemplated it, she began to wonder if the slivers of light represented God trying to reach her through the clutter and distractions she had placed in His way.

The past few months she had definitely been pushing back His light, trying to find comfort within herself, within the shade of arrogance. But, the great thing about God is that He never gives up on us. He placed people, like Brooke and Ruby, and events, like the fireworks display, in Mollie's life to let her know that she was not alone, that she would never be alone. *Fireworks! I forgot to ask Ruby about that song!*

Mollie quickly dialed Ruby's number.

"Hello?"

"Hi Ruby, it's Mollie."

"Well, I'll be! I didn't recognize your number! What a treat to get to talk to you twice today. What's up, Sugar?" she asked with a smile in her voice.

"I was wondering if we could have dinner tonight. There is something I need to ask you," Mollie replied.

123

"Actually, I was about to go get some lunch. I was running late this morning and didn't have time to make something. I am working a longer shift today so my lunch break is for a whole hour. Would you like to get together in about an hour?"

"That would be wonderful! Where would you like to meet?"

"How about the little coffee shop just down the road from the shelter?"

"Perfect! See you in an hour!"

As soon as she was off the phone with Ruby, Mollie dialed Brooke's number. Derek answered.

"Hi Derek. How's Brooke?"

"She's sleeping right now. She didn't get much rest last night," he answered. It sounded like he was exhausted too.

"Would it be okay if I came over in a couple of hours instead of right now?" Mollie asked, hating to be away from Brooke in her time of need.

"Of course. Maybe send us a text when you are on your way."

"I will. See you soon."

Mollie arrived at the coffee shop first and found a table near a window. The lights in the room paled in comparison to the sunlight streaming in. She felt its warmth on her face as she looked up toward the sky. She was lost in the moment when suddenly she felt a hand gently touch her shoulder. Mollie spun around to see Ruby standing there. They hugged and quickly placed their orders.

"I have been scratching my brain for the past hour, wondering what your question is," Ruby said, her eyes dancing.

"Well, I realized that this morning I only told you about Brooke. I didn't tell you about my experience," Mollie said, noticing Ruby's eyes grow wider. "You see, for the past couple of months I have shut everyone out of my life. I have even pushed God away. I felt betrayed by Brooke and her family. First, she didn't tell me about the visits, then the pregnancy and the last straw was when her husband, Derek, called to tell me about the letters they planned to write to the judge asking that Blake's sentence be reduced and that he be set free.

"I was afraid to come to you because I thought you would judge me for ever having had feelings for Blake. I let my pride take over and convince me that I am better off alone. During those months I had this false sense of happiness. I was completely unaware of the damage I was doing. Last night I went for a run by myself because Buster had injured his foot. I thought I had selected my 'Run' folder on my iPod. But, as I was running, I didn't recognize the songs that were playing. One of the songs spoke about God not giving us more than we can take, just like your counselor talked about.

"Just as that song finished I discovered I was running by the baseball stadium because the sky instantly came alive with their beautiful post-game fireworks display. At that very moment a song came on about God lighting up the sky. Ruby, this was no coincidence. These events were orchestrated perfectly by God to let me know that I wasn't alone, that I have never been, nor ever will be. In that moment, I felt His presence and I felt a weight being lifted off my shoulders. I ran home, grabbed Buster and drove to my in-laws' house. My plan was to apologize to all the people I had pushed away, starting with them. I had no idea that Brooke and Derek were there. If it hadn't been for that moment at the stadium I would still be keeping others at a distance and unknowingly leaving Brooke to go through this trying time without me by her side.

"I heard those songs because of you. I had downloaded all the songs on your list and put them in a folder labeled 'Ruby.' I must have accidentally selected your folder when I set out last night for my run. It is a miracle Ruby. *You* are a miracle. So, my question is, why did you have the song about God lighting up the sky on your list?" Mollie asked hesitantly.

Ruby's eyes drifted toward the window, her tears glistening in the sunlight. As they silently fell she told Mollie her reason.

"There is something I didn't tell you when I shared Junior's story. You see, the night before that dreadful day I had been out shopping and came home to find James and Junior already asleep. I had found the most adorable red, white and blue outfit for Junior to

125

wear later that week at his first Fourth of July fireworks show. Like most mothers, I would get excited whenever my baby was about to celebrate a first. So, naturally, I couldn't wait to show James in the morning. To this day I am haunted by it. I've wondered over and over if James wouldn't have been so late leaving that day if I hadn't bothered him with looking at that silly outfit. Perhaps..."

Mollie reached for her hand, feeling guilty for bringing up something so personal, so raw. "Ruby, I am so sorry. This wasn't the place to ask..."

"It's okay," she whispered as she wiped away the tears. "You had no way of knowing. You see, tomorrow is the two year anniversary of Junior's birthday in Heaven. Last year was difficult, but we focused on the celebration of his life, here on Earth and in Heaven. This year we won't have our friends and family surrounding us. It's just James and me," she added as new tears emerged.

"No it's not. You have me," Mollie said, squeezing Ruby's hand as tears streamed down her cheeks.

Mollie promised to spend the Fourth of July with Ruby and James. They would celebrate the lives of the ones they love. Not only would this be the second anniversary of Junior's arrival in Heaven, but it would have also been Mollie's one year wedding anniversary with Brett. God knew how much Ruby and Mollie needed each other. And, thanks to His unconditional love and impeccable timing, they were reunited and their friendship stronger than ever.

CHAPTER THIRTY-TWO

As hard as he tried, Blake could not stop thinking about Mollie. He assured Ruby and James that he had moved on, but he had a feeling that they didn't believe him. The only time when Mollie wasn't on his mind was when he was asleep, or when Sara visited the shelter.

Sara first visited the shelter to drop off a stray dog she had found on her way to work. Her kindness and genuine concern for the dog captured Blake's attention. He could tell that she hated to leave, but she needed to get to work. So, she gave Blake her cell number and asked him to let her know if the dog and his owner were reunited.

Blake thought about texting her after they had tracked down Riley's owner but, instead, he dialed her number. He got her voice mail and left a message. He was surprised when he got a call later that night. He didn't recognize the number but he knew the voice as soon as she spoke.

"Hi Blake. It's Sara. I just wanted to thank you for taking the time to call me. I am so thankful that Riley is back home," she said, a hint of nervousness in her voice.

"Of course. If it hadn't been for you, Riley might still be out there, lost and alone. Thank you for taking the time to bring him in today."

"I was wondering," she paused, "if...the shelter needs any help, like volunteers?" Blake couldn't shake the feeling that she was going to ask something else but changed her mind.

"We are always in need of help. We have volunteers who come in to bathe the animals and people can stop by anytime and walk the dogs. Why do you ask?"

"Well, you see, I am an animal lover, but both of my parents are anti-pets. Spending that brief time with Riley made me wish I could spend more time with animals like him. So, I can just show up at the shelter and walk dogs?" she asked.

"Yep. They just ask for your driver's license and hand you a leash. The reason they ask for your license is so that you are less likely to forget to give back the leash before you leave," Blake added, noticing his palms beginning to sweat.

"Great! I have the day off tomorrow. Maybe I'll stop by. Will you be there?" she asked sheepishly.

"Yep. I am there every day except Sunday."

"Wonderful! Well, I better go. Maybe I'll see you tomorrow. Thanks again Blake!"

"Thank *you* Sara! See you soon," he said as he hung up the phone.

Blake sat back in his chair. That was when he noticed his heart racing. *What is wrong with me? How could I be getting so worked up over someone I have known for only five minutes? Is there a reason why she asked if I would be at the shelter tomorrow?* Blake shook his head. *She probably just wants a familiar face to show her around, that's all.*

The next day, Blake was busy feeding some of the dogs when he felt someone gently touch his arm. He spun around to find Sara standing next to him, a shy smile on her face. The warmth of her touch and the beauty of her smile caught Blake off guard.

"Hi!" he said as he set the bag of dog food down, trying to mask his nervousness.

"Hi! I was hoping you were here. I have my leash. Any suggestions for who I should walk first? Break me in gently," she chuckled.

Blake laughed. He was surprised at how natural it felt. He couldn't remember the last time he laughed. *Oh wait, it was with...*

"Well, let's see. Cookie is a pretty gentle dog," he suggested.

"Cookie, huh? Maybe after I am done walking her I can take Cupcake or Truffles out next," she giggled and bumped Blake's arm with her elbow.

"I'll have them waiting for you when you get back," he joked, unable to suppress his smile.

"Well, gee, thanks," she added as she took Cookie out of her kennel.

"Have fun!" he shouted as Sara and Cookie made their way to the hallway.

"We will! See you soon!" she yelled back over her shoulder and gave a little wink.

Blake bent down to pick up the bag of dog food and realized that his hands were trembling. *Maybe my blood sugar is low. No...that's not it. This girl is having an effect on me. So much has happened in the past six months and my heart has already revealed how eager it is to find love again when I met Mollie. I better keep my distance, at least for now. Besides, if she knew my story she would probably run the other way. Mollie did.*

W

As much as Blake tried to keep his distance, Sara seemed determined to spend time with him whenever she volunteered at the shelter. Through their conversations, he learned that she was going to be a junior in the fall at the local college. He guessed that she was twenty, maybe even twenty-one. Blake was about to turn twenty-seven so they weren't that far apart, age wise. But when it came to life experiences, they were worlds apart.

He was thankful that Sara didn't ask him too many questions. *Maybe I should just tell her the truth. She'll be shocked and probably have some sudden reason why she can no longer volunteer. Besides, even with someone to spend time with, I can't keep my mind off of Mollie. This isn't fair to anybody.*

CHAPTER THIRTY-THREE

Each day Mollie prayed for God to miraculously heal Brooke's baby girl. One night she opened up her Bible to reread the book of James. She was ashamed that she had stopped going to Bible study. Instead of surrounding herself with people who loved her and being filled with the Word of God, she pulled away and let her foolish pride have control.

She read James 4:15. "Instead, you ought to say, 'If it is the Lord's will, we will live and do this or that. [36]'" Suddenly it occurred to Mollie just how arrogant she had been. *She* had been making plans, like quitting her job and preparing to move, without first consulting God. She knelt beside her bed and prayed, "Lord, I am so sorry for not seeking You first with all of my decisions and my actions. Please forgive me. From now on, I submit myself to Your will and Your plan for my life. I cannot undo the past, but I give You my future. Your Word says that our lives are but a mist. [37] Please guide me to make the most of my mist. And Lord, I pray that if it is Your will, that you would heal Brooke's baby. But, if it is not, then I pray for Your hand of comfort and peace upon Brooke and Derek, especially in the coming months. And, it is my fervent prayer that, if their baby is not healed, that Brooke and Derek will get to have some time with her before she passes from this world and enters Your Heavenly Kingdom. Amen."

Mollie could taste the salt from her tears as she stood up. She would give anything for Brooke's baby to be healthy. Yet, she couldn't shake the feeling that there would be no miracle; that Brooke's baby would not be healed. *Lord, please help me help Brooke. She needs You, now more than ever...*

W

Blake had started getting used to seeing Sara at the shelter. So, it was no surprise when he saw her walking in as he was making his way to the front door, Honey tugging at the leash. As soon as she saw him her face lit up. Blake had to admit, his did too.

"Hey there! Mind if I walk with you?" she asked excitedly.

"The more the merrier," he replied.

"Great! Would it be okay if I quick run back and get Cookie?"

"Sure. Honey and I will be waiting outside."

Soon they were on their way up the dirt road near the shelter. Blake couldn't help but notice the majesty of creation all around them. The crystal blue sky, the lush green meadows scattered with wild flowers and the sun, embracing them with its warmth.

"Looks like the start of a perfect summer day," he said, trying to break the awkward silence.

"Mmm, hmmm," Sara said, seemingly unable to come up with something more to say in response.

"Any big plans before classes start up again?" Blake asked, desperately trying to make conversation.

"Not really. I am a lifeguard at the waterpark, and this is our busiest time of the season so no one really has much of a chance to take time off. But that's okay. I am really looking forward to school starting again. I can't wait to start my practicum," she said as they made the turn to head back toward the shelter.

"What is a practicum?"

"Oh, I'm sorry. I am so used to hearing that word that I forget that others may not be familiar with it. I am working toward a degree in elementary education. A practicum is when we have a chance to work with a teacher in his or her classroom. We learn ways to manage the classroom, create lesson plans, stuff like that, to prepare us for when we do our student teaching. Student teaching is the last step before graduating."

"Oh, so it is kind of like an internship?" Blake asked.

"Exactly! I was hoping to work with a specific teacher this fall. She is such a sweetheart and everyone raves about her. But I just heard that she is moving away so it looks like I have to find someone else to work with," Sara added, a hint of disappointment in her voice.

"I'm sorry to hear that. I am sure there are lots of excellent teachers to choose from," he mentioned, trying to cheer her up.

"There are. But there was just something about Mollie Walker. We met when I was doing a small practicum with one of her co-workers. We hit it off instantly. Oh well, I guess it just wasn't meant to be," Sara said as she shrugged her shoulders.

Did she just say Mollie Walker? And did she say that Mollie is moving away?! Blake's heart broke as those words sank in. *Is she moving to get away from all of the memories or from...me?* He did his best to fake a smile as they finished their walk. He was thankful that Sara had to leave for work. He needed some time alone to process things; to finally come to terms with the fact that Mollie would never be in his life again...

Ruby couldn't help but notice the way that Sara looked at Blake. And, Ruby could tell that Blake enjoyed Sara's company but was keeping his heart guarded. *Sara has been such a breath of fresh air, so full of life. Maybe she is just what Blake needs; especially after all he has been through.*

Blake hadn't mentioned Mollie in weeks, but he wasn't fooling Ruby. She could sense that he still longed for her. And, when Mollie stopped by the shelter a few weeks ago, Ruby could tell that Brooke's news wasn't the only thing tugging at Mollie's heartstrings.

Ruby assumed that Mollie knew about the early release since she mentioned the letters to the judge. And ever since their lunch at the coffee shop, Ruby has thought about telling Mollie that Blake now works at the shelter. But she decided to mind her tongue, and her business. Yet, it was difficult to watch two dear friends seem so alone. *Dear Lord, please help Blake and Mollie. I can't help but think that they are meant to be together. But, if that is not Your will, then please help them find someone to love again.*

Ruby opened her eyes to see Blake standing in front of her.

"I'm so sorry Ruby. I didn't disturb you, did I?"

"Not at all Sugar. Just talking to God," she replied with a huge grin.

Blake flashed that handsome smile and handed Ruby several pieces of paper.

"What's this?" she asked.

"It's my testimony. I was wondering if you and James would read it and give me some feedback. I'm not exactly comfortable speaking in front of people, but I guess that is something I'll have to work on," he said, a hint of nervousness in his voice.

"And pray about," Ruby chimed in. "We would be honored to read this. James and I will read it together as soon as we get home. Why don't you come over for dinner tonight so we can discuss it further?"

"That would be wonderful! Thank you so much Ruby! I really appreciate this!" Blake said as he wrapped his arms around her.

Ruby quickly texted James and asked if he could come home a little early today. They have some important reading to do.

CHAPTER THIRTY-FOUR

On the drive to Ruby's, Blake felt himself growing more and more anxious. He desperately wanted to know what they thought of his testimony and at the same time feared what they would say. Throughout his message, Blake exposed so much of himself and what happened that day. He considered himself to be a private person, and it was stretching him beyond his limits to share such intimate details with friends, let alone complete strangers. Ruby was right; Blake would need God's help to get him through this.

He felt his body shaking as he rang their doorbell. Ruby must have seen him pull into the driveway because the door immediately opened. In an instant Blake could tell she had been crying. She stepped forward and threw her arms around him.

"Ruby, are you okay? What's wrong?"

She pulled back and looked deep into Blake's eyes. "Oh Blake, we just finished reading your testimony," she whispered. "It's...it's..." She began crying, unable to speak.

"It's that bad?" he asked, the expression on his face begging her to answer.

"Not at all! We can see God's hand in all of it! You are going to change lives with your story! We can feel it," she exclaimed as tears, once again, gathering in the corner of her eyes.

Blake looked up as James entered the room. In silence, James walked toward him. Blake could tell that he wanted to say something but could not find the words. Instead, James reached out and hugged him. "We are so proud of you," James whispered.

Over dinner, Blake told Ruby and James that his first speaking engagement was on Sunday at one of the local churches. Immediately Ruby asked if it would be okay for them to come.

Blake's parents had asked to attend too. The idea of having friends or family there, especially with this being his first time, made Blake's stomach ache. But as much as Blake liked the idea of speaking to only strangers, he knew he would need a support system there with him.

$$W$$

When Sunday came, Blake was a nervous wreck. He paced the hallway by the sanctuary, waiting to be told to go in. He looked down at his already trembling hands. As more and more time went by, the uneasy feeling in his stomach was becoming unbearable. *How am I ever going to get through this?*

Before the service, Ruby, James and his parents had poured into him with their words of encouragement. Ruby even offered to pray over Blake before they went in to sit down. *Pray! That's what I should be doing! There is no way I am going to make it through this without God's help!*

"Dear Lord, I need You. Please speak through me. I can't do this alone. Amen."

"Blake, it's time," a young woman said from the doorway.

As Blake walked along the side of the stage he thought he would faint, or possibly be sick. His whole body was shaking. *Please Lord help me! Please!* All Blake heard as he walked onto the stage was his name and people clapping.

The thought of seeing all those faces staring back at him was what troubled Blake the most. As he made his way to the podium, he discovered that the spotlights shining down onto the stage provided most of the light in the sanctuary which meant that the majority of the audience was hidden in a cloud of darkness. *Thank You Lord!*

As Blake spoke, he slowly felt his nervousness subside. His emotions, however, were another story. As hard as he tried, it was impossible to fight back the tears. The events were still fresh, the pain raw. Most of that first speaking engagement was a blur. All he remembered saying was, "Thank you," and seeing people begin to stand up and applaud. That's when Blake lost it and felt the pastor's arms wrap around him. He looked Blake in the eyes and said, "Well done, good and faithful servant.[38]"

As much as Blake wanted to leave after exposing so much, the pastor asked if he would stay after the service for those who may have questions or want to talk with him. Blake wanted to say no, but he felt this nudging to stay.

As soon as the pastor finished his closing remarks, people began walking toward the stage instead of toward the doors. It was overwhelming but, thankfully, Blake's parents and Ruby and James stood by him the whole time. Responses ranged from hugs, to words of encouragement, to people sharing their stories of loss or regret. Before he knew it, an hour had come and gone. He was exhausted, in every sense of the word, and it must have been obvious to the others.

"Honey, let's go home and I'll make you some lunch," his mom offered, a look of concern on her face.

"Blake, we are so proud of you. We just know that God is going to do some amazing things through you," Ruby added as she gave him a big hug.

After lunch, Blake went to his room. He needed some time to himself and some rest. As he lay in bed, the events of the day replayed in his mind. Even with so much to reflect on, one thing kept interrupting his thoughts...Mollie. *Where is she? Does she still hate me? Will she ever forgive me? Could she ever...?*

CHAPTER THIRTY-FIVE

As the weeks went by, Brooke and Derek began planning for their daughter's birth. Because their baby would not likely survive a natural birth, the doctors scheduled a C-section at thirty-eight weeks. That was only two months away, and Mollie had a feeling that it would be the longest two months of Brooke's life.

After careful consideration and prayer, Brooke and Derek decided to move closer to her parents. Derek was able to find a job right away and, even though there were several openings for nurses at the local hospitals, Brooke decided to take a leave, at least for now.

"Part of me feels like I am being a coward, that I should face this situation head on. But, the fact is, that with my job, I am constantly coming in contact with strangers. Numerous times throughout the day someone would ask about my pregnancy. Before the diagnosis I loved answering their questions. Now, it feels like I am ripping a bandage off a fresh wound every time I talk about our baby."

"You are the farthest thing from a coward. You're one of the strongest people I have ever known," Mollie replied as she reached for Brooke's hands.

"Thank you for being here for me, for us. I don't know what I would do without you," Brooke said, squeezing Mollie's hands.

"Or Buster," Mollie teased and gave her a little wink.

Brooke smiled and looked down at Buster who was sprawled out over her lap. "He is an amazing dog. Wherever did you find him?" she asked.

Her question caught Mollie off guard. "I found him at the shelter. Someone recommended him," she said dryly as her eyes started to glisten.

"Oh Mollie! I'm so sorry. It was…" Brooke didn't need to finish. She already knew the answer.

"How about we go for a walk?" Mollie suggested. Buster sprung up and bolted for the door. They couldn't help but laugh. *Brooke is right; he really is an amazing dog.*

Later that night, Mollie struggled to fall asleep. Her mind kept replaying a conversation she had with Brooke earlier in the day. Brooke had mentioned that she and Derek planned to live with her parents, at least for a little while, since she would not be working. Although Brooke was thankful for a place to stay, Mollie could tell that she and Derek would rather have a place of their own.

Suddenly, Mollie knew what to do. She had been angry at herself for making such rash decisions like quitting her job and not renewing her lease without first consulting God. But, as only God can, He was showing her how He can use *her* actions for *His* perfect plan. Mollie couldn't wait to see Brooke in the morning.

The next day, Brooke could sense Mollie's excitement as soon as she walked into the living room. Buster must have sensed something too because he instantly jumped up on Brooke's lap and covered her in kisses.

"You two sure seem to be in a good mood," Brooke chuckled.

Mollie sat down next to Brooke, unable to suppress her smile. "Brooke, I have been doing some thinking and I want to run something by you. As you know, I resigned from my teaching job and did not renew the lease on my apartment. My plan is to move back home and live with my parents."

"I know. I'm really going to miss having you around," Brooke whispered, fighting back tears.

"You said that you and Derek will be staying with your parents for a while, until you go back to work. But, I know you too well. As kind as it is of your parents to open their home to you, you would prefer to have a place of your own."

"You're right. You do know me well," she admitted.

"I think I have a solution that would allow you and Derek to get a place of your own and also give you as much time as you need until you are ready to go back to work," Mollie said as butterflies burst in her stomach.

"How?"

"Well, after Brett's death, I used some of his life insurance policy to cover the funeral expenses. The rest I have put away in savings. If you and Derek find an apartment, or even a house, I could help out until you are ready to go back to work."

"Oh Mollie, we couldn't. That's too much..."

"But I'm not finished," Mollie added with a grin. "You see, come the end of this month I will be homeless and I don't want to leave you either, especially right now. That means that Buster and I would need somewhere to stay while we wait on your little one to arrive. So, really, you would be helping me out and I would be paying you rent. So...what do you say to having a couple of roommates for the next few months?"

"Oh Mollie! That is the best idea ever! I would love for you to live with us, and Buster too," she added, scratching him behind the ears. "This is such an answer to our prayers!"

"There's more. I have something for you," Mollie said as she reached into her purse. She pulled out a small journal. On the cover were two mountains, one to the left and one on the right. Between the two mountains was a valley. The mountains were gray and bare. The valley was lush and beautiful. Below the picture it read, "Life is full of peaks and valleys. We long for the peaks, but growth only happens in the valleys.[39] 'So do not fear, for I am with you; do not be dismayed, for I am your God. I will strengthen you and help you; I will uphold you with my righteous right hand.[40]'"

Tears fell from Brooke's cheeks as she opened the journal. She silently read the message Mollie had written on the first page.

Brooke,

No matter what happens in our lives, God is always there for us. As you turn to God, may your heart be filled with His peace and hope, now and forever.

"Do not be anxious about anything, but in every situation, by prayer and petition, with thanksgiving, present your requests to God. And the peace of God, which transcends all understanding, will guard your hearts and your minds in Christ Jesus.[41]"

"And we know that in all things God works for the good of those who love Him, who have been called according to His purpose.[17]"

Love,
Mollie

Brooke then carefully turned to the page with the tab 'Worry.' She read the verses out loud as her voice, and her body, trembled.

"1 Peter 5:7: Cast all your anxiety on Him because He cares for you.[42] John 14:27: Peace I leave with you; My peace I give to you. Not as the world gives do I give to you. Let not your hearts be troubled, neither let them be afraid.[43] Psalm 56:3: When I am afraid, I put my trust in You.[44] Proverbs 3:5: Trust in the Lord with all your heart, and lean not on your own understanding.[3]"

She reached for a pen on the coffee table and began writing. When she was finished, she handed the journal to Mollie.

"Psalm 23:4: Even though I walk through the valley of the shadow of death, I will fear no evil, for You are with me; Your rod and Your staff, they comfort me,[45]" Mollie read aloud.

It was this exact verse that Mollie was too afraid to write down in the journal. She wasn't sure how Brooke would react to those words. Brooke was definitely going through a valley, a valley of death. Not only had she lost her only brother but now she was awaiting the birth, and death, of her baby girl. If there was anything left of Mollie's broken heart it was being torn apart over the pain her beloved friend was enduring. *Lord, please wrap Your arms around her. She desperately needs to feel You, to know You are near.*

CHAPTER THIRTY-SIX

Between helping Derek and Brooke pack up their apartment and packing up her own, Mollie felt like she was constantly on the go, running from one place to the next. Today was no exception. She grabbed her keys for what would hopefully be her last trip to the grocery store for empty boxes. She ran down the steps of her apartment complex and threw open the door to the building. She was in such a hurry that she didn't see that there was a man standing next to the door. In her haste, Mollie had almost knocked him over.

"Ms. Walker?" he asked. There was something familiar about his voice.

The shock of the situation began to fade, but Mollie still couldn't place his voice; that face.

The confused look on her face gave her away. "Ma'am, I'm Officer Cooper. I was the one who delivered the accident report," he continued, a hint of regret in his voice.

"Of course," she replied, catching her breath. *No wonder I didn't remember right away, he's not in uniform.* "I am so sorry for opening the door like that. Are you okay?" she asked hesitantly.

"Yes Ma'am," he said with a smile. "I am actually here to see you. I just buzzed your apartment but there was no answer. I guess you must have just walked out the door, or should I say, ran?"

"In hind sight, I *should* have walked," Mollie chuckled. "You said you are here to see *me*?"

"Yes Ma'am. You see, I was updating some paperwork when I came across your file. I discovered that the other driver was recently granted an early release. That is quite rare in situations such as yours. I thought I would check in with you and see how you are doing."

"He's been released? How long has he been out?" she asked, trying to process this new information.

"A little over a month."

Mollie's mind was reeling. *He has been out for over a month? Why didn't Brooke say anything? Why hasn't Ruby said something?*

Officer Cooper sensed her alarm. "Ma'am, would you like to grab some coffee and talk?"

"Sure," Mollie managed to say, her voice wavering.

"My truck is right over here if you would like to ride together," he offered. Mollie noticed a hint of nervousness in his voice.

"I'm so sorry for not recognizing you right away," she said as she climbed into his truck. "I think it threw me off that you are not in uniform."

"No need to apologize. Today is my day off. Hence, no uniform," he said with a smile that was utterly contagious.

He came to see me on his day off? Why? He could have easily called instead to see how I am doing.

Over coffee, Officer Cooper provided more details about the release. Mollie learned that Blake is on probation for the next two years and is required to tell his story at churches, schools and various organizations during that time in the hopes that it will keep the memories fresh in his mind and prevent him, and anyone who hears his story, from making the same mistake.

Mollie was flooded with a mix of emotions. She felt betrayed, wondering why Brooke and Ruby would keep this from her. She was angry that he was free to live his life and Brett could not. And yet, somehow, she found herself feeling concerned for Blake. She thought about how difficult it must be to not only live with the fact that he took someone's life but to also have to admit it to others and relive it over and over again.

A look of remorse came over Officer Cooper's face. "Ma'am..."

"Please, call me Mollie" she said, trying to smile as she fought back tears.

"Mollie, I...I thought you already knew about his early release. I didn't mean to...to give you difficult news, again," he said, unable to look her in the eyes.

"Officer Cooper-"

"Please, call me John," he said, his kind eyes staring back at her.

"John, over the past few months I have gained a deeper understanding that everything happens for a reason; even if I cannot comprehend what that reason might be. As difficult as some of this information has been to take in, I am thankful to have someone as kind as you to be the one to share it with me. It was very thoughtful of you to take the time to check in on me," Mollie said, suddenly feeling a nervous energy pulsating through her body.

"It is the least I could do. And, if you ever need someone to talk to please don't hesitate to call."

"Thank you. I may just take you up on that offer," she joked.

"I hope you do," he said, looking deep into her eyes.

Mollie felt her cheeks growing warm. She had hoped that he didn't notice her blushing but the smile on his face told her otherwise.

"So, where were you running off to when we bumped into each other?" John asked as they drove back to her apartment complex.

"Oh! That's right! I was on my way to the grocery store to get more empty boxes," Mollie replied.

"Empty boxes?"

"Yes. I am moving in a week and I have a few more things left to pack up. Hopefully the grocery store still has some boxes left by the time I get there."

"Oh," he replied, trying to mask his disappointment.

"I am moving in with my sister-in-law and her husband. They are buying a house on the west side of town."

"Oh," he said with a new found excitement. "Need any help moving your things?"

"I think I have enough helpers lined up. Thanks for the offer though," she said as she stepped out of his truck.

He reached into his glove box and handed Mollie something. She looked down to discover it was his business card. On the front he had written his cell phone number.

"Please be sure to give me a call if you ever need anything," he said. Mollie couldn't shake the feeling that he didn't want to leave.

"I will. Thanks so much John," she replied, not wanting him to leave either.

Little did she know just how soon she would see him again.

CHAPTER THIRTY-SEVEN

Ever since that night by the baseball stadium, Mollie had been trying desperately to learn from her mistakes; to not let her pride and anger get the better of her. But, it was proving to be more challenging than she had anticipated. After learning about Blake's release, she was instantly angry at Ruby and Brooke. *Why didn't they tell me?* The words of James echoed in her mind, "...be quick to listen, slow to speak and slow to anger.[10]" *There has to be an explanation. I need to get to the bottom of this.*

The next morning, Mollie texted Ruby and asked her to call when she had some free time. Mollie was surprised when her phone suddenly started ringing.

"Wow! That was quick," Mollie said as she answered.

"I just happen to be on my morning break. What's up, Sugar?"

Mollie knew she didn't have much time so she got right to the point. "Ruby, why didn't you tell me that Blake was released?"

"Oh Sugar, I thought you knew! That day when we had lunch together you mentioned the letters your in-laws wrote to the judge. I just assumed you knew the end result. I'm so sorry!" she exclaimed and Mollie could tell that she was genuinely surprised.

"It's okay. I just found out yesterday and I couldn't figure out why you haven't said anything about it. It all makes sense now."

"I'm so sorry Mollie! I shouldn't have made such an assumption. I should have talked to you about it right away."

"Really, it's okay. I'll admit that when I first heard the news, I was angry. I felt betrayed and wanted to turn inward and shut everyone out like I've done before. But even though it felt natural, I knew it was wrong. Now, more than ever, I am aware of the constant battle raging between my sinful nature and the way God intends for me to live. So, instead of letting my feelings have control over me I picked up the phone and texted you. And, I'm so glad I did."

"Me too, Sugar! I have to get back to work but I promise...no more assumptions"

"Me too! Thanks Ruby! Talk to you soon," Mollie said as she hung up.

A wave of relief came over Mollie. Ruby hadn't been the only one to make assumptions. Mollie had assumed that Ruby was keeping this information from her, but that was the farthest thing from the truth. Now she started to wonder if Brooke knew about Blake's release. Mollie decided to call Derek first.

"Hi Mollie. Is everything okay?" Derek asked immediately.

"Hi Derek. Yes, everything is fine. I just have a question for you," she said, her stomach twisting in knots.

"Oh good! For a moment there, I thought something was wrong with Brooke, or our baby," he said, a sense of relief in his voice.

"Oh Derek, I'm so sorry for scaring you! Next time I will text you before I call so you know it isn't an emergency," she said, suddenly feeling sick to her stomach.

"I'm sorry too. I guess I'm a little on edge. These past months have definitely tested my ability to trust God and know that He is in control. I'd like to say that I'm not worried, but that would be a lie. Every day I worry about our baby and whether we will get to have time with her before she goes to be with Jesus. And, I am constantly worrying about Brooke. She is trying to be so strong, but I can tell that her pain is beyond anything I can comprehend. Her growing belly and ever active baby are constant reminders of the life, and death, that are to come. The not knowing is really taking a toll on her, and on me," he said, his voice wavering.

"Oh Derek! I'm so sorry!"

"Somehow, God will help us through this," he said, desperately trying to regain his composure. "You...you said you have a question for me."

"Oh, that's right! A couple of months ago you told me about the letters you wrote on Blake's behalf...for an early release."

"Oh! I guess with everything going on I had kind of forgotten all about them," he said apologetically.

"Have you heard anything since writing them? Did he get released?"

"I'm sorry, Mollie. I don't know. We planned to look into it but..." his voice trailed off.

"Oh Derek, please don't be sorry. Your focus needs to be on Brooke and your baby."

"I could look into it for you," he offered.

"Actually, I already know the answer. The officer who delivered the accident report stopped by yesterday and told me that Blake was released about five weeks ago."

"He's been out for over a month?" Derek asked in disbelief.

"That is what the officer said. At first I assumed you all knew and didn't tell me. But, after my past mistakes I have learned not to jump to conclusions. So, instead, I picked up the phone and called you."

"I'm so glad you did. And, thank you for calling me instead of Brooke. Lately, we have been trying to minimize her stress levels. We desperately want her pregnancy to continue as long as possible so our baby girl will have at least *some* chance of surviving, if only for a little while. I will be sure to tell her though. She will be thankful to know that our prayer has been answered."

Their prayer has been answered... His words resonated in Mollie's mind and deep in her heart. *Lord, You graciously answered their prayer for Blake. Will You not also answer their prayer for their baby girl? Oh Lord, may it be Your will to heal her!*

"I'm praying for you, all of you," Mollie said, tears streaming down her face.

"Thank you Mollie. We need all the prayer we can get."

"Are we still on for Wednesday afternoon?" she asked, trying to lighten the conversation.

"Oh Mollie! I totally forgot! The doctors scheduled another ultrasound Wednesday afternoon so I won't be able to help you move your couch. Is there anyone else who might be able to help?"

"I think so. Don't worry about a thing. You just focus on Brooke and your baby."

"Thanks Mollie, for everything," he replied as he hung up.

Mollie's stomach instantly filled with butterflies as she began dialing his number.

"Hello?" he said after the third ring.

"Hi Officer Cooper. This is Mollie Walker," she said nervously.

"Well, this is a pleasant surprise! And, please, call me John," he said tenderly.

"Oh, I'm sorry. Seems to be a hard habit to break," she joked.

"I'm so glad you called. The number we had listed in your file appears to have been disconnected," he replied.

What a fool I am! He didn't stop by the other day because he wanted to see me! It was because he had no other way to reach me.

"Oh, I forgot about that. I changed my number a few months ago. That explains why you stopped by my apartment the other day. I'm so sorry for taking up your time like that," she said apologetically.

"Who said that was my only reason for stopping by?" he teased, but Mollie got the distinct feeling that he wasn't joking.

She immediately began blushing and was thankful that they were not face to face.

"Remember when you asked if I would need any help with the move?" Mollie asked hesitantly.

"Mmmm, hmmm," he answered. She could tell that he was smiling.

"Well, a teacher friend of mine bought my couch and I told her I would drop it off on Wednesday afternoon. My brother-in-law was going to help me, but something has come up. I know this is very short notice and I completely understand if-"

"Mollie, I would love to," he interrupted. "And, your timing is perfect. I work the night shift on Wednesday. So, I can help move your couch before heading into work. What time should I stop by?"

"Would four o'clock be okay? It shouldn't take too long. I really appreciate this!" she said, her heart racing.

"Four o'clock it is. And, I know how you can make it up to me. How about we grab a bite to eat together after we deliver the couch?" he suggested.

"It's a deal," she replied, trying to contain her excitement.

"Great! I will see you on Wednesday at four o'clock."

"Wonderful! Thank you so much... for everything."

CHAPTER THIRTY-EIGHT

Often, Blake has heard people say, "Time flies when you're having fun." As true as that statement may be, his motto lately has been, "Time flies when you are busy." Of course there have been brief moments when he has experienced joy but they have been few and far between. Instead, his weeks have been filled with work, speaking engagements, and...Sara.

Word spread quickly after Blake first shared his testimony. He began receiving numerous calls from churches wanting to schedule a visit. Suddenly, every Sunday through December was booked and schools began scheduling visits during the week as well.

The more Blake gave his testimony, the more at ease he felt standing in front of large groups of people. And instead of wanting to bolt as soon as he was finished, he looked forward to spending time after the service talking with people and listening to their stories. Those were the moments when he felt the most connected to others; that he wasn't alone. It was at night, or when he had some quiet time to himself, that he would think of Mollie and suddenly feel incomplete.

The more Blake worked at the shelter, the more he saw it as an answer to prayer. He needed the unconditional love these animals gave so freely. They filled him with such joy and he couldn't help but pour it right back into them. He devoted a lot of attention to the animals who had been at the shelter a long time. Some of them had been there for over one hundred days. Blake could relate. He knew what it was like to be caged- to long for freedom... and love.

"You certainly have a way with animals," Sara noted during one of her visits.

"Thanks," Blake chuckled. "I guess I feel a kind of connection with them. Sounds silly, I know."

"It doesn't sound silly at all. You are a blessing to these animals. Your being here is probably the highlight of their day," she said, looking deep into his eyes.

Blake felt his body suddenly grow warm and quickly turned toward one of the kennels.

"I guess we need each other," he said as he bent down and scratched Bruno behind the ears.

"We all need someone," she added, gently touching his shoulder.

Her words spoke to his very soul. Ultimately, all we *really* need is God. Yet, many of us have this need, this longing, to also share our lives with someone here on Earth. As much as Blake tried to suppress this desire, it would bubble up to the surface over and over again.

Have You brought Sara into my life for a reason? Is she here to help me get over Mollie? Is it Your will for us to be together? Lord, please show me!

The more time Sara and Blake spent together the more he sensed her feelings for him growing deeper. He could tell that his feelings for her were deepening too but he was still guarding his heart. *She doesn't know my story. If she did, she wouldn't be here.*

CHAPTER THIRTY-NINE

Each passing day brought excitement, and anxiety, about the birth of Brooke's baby. To ease the tension, Brooke and Mollie would take Buster for a walk every day. It was one of the rare times when Brooke would leave the house. During their walks they would quietly take in the beauty of creation all around them.

"It's overwhelming, isn't it?" Brooke asked.

"What?" Mollie asked, unsure of what she was referring to.

"That all of this was created by God. Sometimes my mind struggles to grasp the fact that not only did God create everything we see, but He also knows the number of hairs on each person's head," she said, staring up at the sky.

"I know. It is beyond our comprehension. To think that He created all this, knows everything about each of us, *and* loves us unconditionally seems impossible. But nothing is impossible with God,⁹" Mollie replied, looking at her.

Brooke gently placed her hands on her stomach as tears welled up in her eyes.

"Oh Brooke! I'm so sorry! I..."

"Mollie, it's okay. Every moment of every day I have been praying that God would miraculously heal our little girl. Every time she moves and kicks I wonder how something so alive, so active, still has no chance of survival. Each time we have an ultrasound I pray that the doctors will discover that her condition has suddenly disappeared. Yet, each time we go, the prognosis is the same. At least during our last ultrasound we were able to get an image of her face. It is my most treasured possession."

Mollie immediately walked over and gave Brooke a hug. They stood there, quietly crying together. Even Buster, who is normally tugging at the leash to keep walking, had wrapped himself around their legs. It's moments like these that Mollie will cherish in her heart forever...

W

For the past few weeks, Ruby has been riddled with guilt. She couldn't seem to get over the fact that she had, unknowingly, kept something from Mollie when she didn't tell her about Blake's early release. She felt awful that she had made such an assumption. She could only imagine what Mollie's reaction must have been when she was told the news. And now Ruby wondered if she was doing it again...keeping something from her dear friend. She just had to tell Mollie, no matter what her reaction might be. Ruby prayed that Mollie wouldn't be angry with her for not telling her sooner. Her hands trembled as she dialed Mollie's number.

"Hi Ruby. How are you?" Mollie asked as she answered her phone.

"Well, hello Sugar! I tell ya, I still get caught off guard when someone already knows it's me calling before I even say hello. Silly caller id," she chuckled, trying to conceal her nervousness.

"I know. Guess it can be a blessing and a curse. What's up?"

"Well, I was wondering if we could have lunch together." Ruby waited eagerly for her response.

"Sure! I'd love to. What day would work well for you?" she asked.

"Would you be free today?"

"Sure! Is everything okay?"

"Oh yes, everything is just fine. I am working another long shift and thought it would be nice to have lunch with my dear friend. Should we meet at the little coffee shop in an hour?"

"Perfect! See you soon," Mollie said lightheartedly.

Ruby's stomach felt as if it were tied into a million knots by the time she left for the coffee shop. It would have definitely been easier to tell Mollie over the phone, but she deserved more than that, especially after all she has been through and is now going through with her sister-in-law.

Mollie greeted Ruby outside the café. After placing their orders, they sat down at a little table in the corner.

Ruby couldn't take it anymore. She had to tell her. "Remember when I told you that I would not make assumptions ever again?" Ruby asked, hesitantly.

"Mmmm, hmmm," Mollie replied and Ruby could tell she was wondering where the conversation was going.

"Mollie, there is something I haven't told you," she said, unable to look Mollie in the eyes. "Blake has been working at the shelter ever since his release."

A look of absolute shock came over Mollie.

"He's been working at the shelter, with you, ever since his release?" Mollie asked, utterly bewildered.

"Yes," Ruby whispered.

"Why...why didn't you tell me this sooner?" she asked. The look on her face broke Ruby's heart.

"When I assumed that you knew about his release I also assumed that you knew about him getting a job at the shelter. It was wrong of me to make these assumptions and I want to make things right. I hope I can make things right," Ruby said as she twisted her napkin over and over in her hands.

Mollie sat back in her chair in disbelief.

"I...I think I was scared," Ruby continued. "I was afraid that if I told you that you would be angry with me or that it might be too much all at one time. But, you deserve to know. Even if this affects our friendship."

Mollie leaned forward and gently squeezed Ruby's hand. "Ruby, please don't be upset. I'm glad you told me. If this were a month ago I probably would have stormed out the door. But, spending time with Brooke and witnessing just how fragile life is has shown me that life is too short to hold grudges and harbor unforgiveness. I believe you. I know you wouldn't do something to intentionally hurt me. You were trying to protect me."

"Oh Mollie! Thank you for being so understanding!" Ruby exclaimed, letting the tears come.

"Is... is he doing well?" Mollie asked, somewhat sheepishly.

Her question surprised Ruby. "Um, yes. He is a natural with those animals. We are very fortunate to have had an opening right when he was released. I believe it was Divine Timing."

"Do you get to speak with him often?" Mollie inquired.

Even though a part of Ruby still believed that Mollie had feelings for Blake, she was surprised that Mollie was asking these questions. "We chat occasionally at work, and he has been over for dinner now and then. He and James have developed quite a bond."

"It's nice that he has you and James for support," she said softly.

"Oh, I almost forgot. Do you know a Sara Foster?" Ruby asked. *Why did I just blurt that out?*

"One of the teachers at my school had a practicum student this year named Sara Foster. Why do you ask?"

"Sara has been volunteering a lot at the shelter. I've had a chance to talk with her and she said she is studying to be a teacher. I mentioned your name and she told me that she knew you. She said that she had hoped to work with you this fall but that you are moving. *Are* you moving away?" Ruby asked anxiously.

"I was, but thankfully God has used my rash decisions for His plan. A few months ago, I quit my teaching job and chose not to renew my lease. I planned to move back home and live with my parents for a while until I figured out what to do next. But all of that has changed now. Brooke and Derek decided to move here to be closer to her family, and I moved in with them. I want to be there for Brooke as much as possible, especially before the baby comes. And, as much as I have regretted quitting my job, it has turned out to be a blessing. Even though Brooke is scheduled for a C-section, things could change in an instant. Because I am not teaching I can be ready whenever she needs me."

"That *is* a blessing indeed! And, I'm so glad you aren't moving away!" Ruby exclaimed.

"Me too. I'm not sure what lies ahead. I guess that's where trust comes in," Mollie said with a smile.

"Absolutely, Sugar!" Ruby said, beaming.

"You said that Sara has been volunteering at the shelter?" Mollie asked, her question quickly changing the subject.

"Mmmm, hmmm. She found a stray dog several weeks ago and brought him in. She talked about how she wishes she could have a pet but her parents are against it. Blake told her about all the ways people can volunteer at the shelter and she has been coming by ever since," Ruby replied, noticing the look on Mollie's face change.

"She knows Blake?" she asked.

"Oh yes. They've spent quite a bit of time together," Ruby said, suddenly wishing she could take back her words.

"Well...I'm glad he has found someone to spend time with. She is very sweet," Mollie said with a forced smile.

CHAPTER FORTY

Mollie's mind was racing as she drove home. *What is wrong with me? Why can't I stop thinking about Blake and Sara spending time together? Am I...jealous? This is ridiculous! Besides, John and I have started spending more time together and he is an amazing guy. Lord, please help me. None of this makes sense.*

Mollie shook her head as she parked in front of Brooke and Derek's new home. Right now her focus needed to be on Brooke. Her C-section was only two weeks away, and everyone felt like they were walking on eggshells. The uncertainty of what lie ahead was weighing heavily on all of them. Even with all of their efforts to keep Brooke's stress level down, Mollie could tell that she was anxious.

Although the doctors reassured Brooke that everything was still progressing normally, she began limiting physical activity. Her hope was that it would prolong her pregnancy as much as possible. Mollie missed their walks together. John must have somehow sensed it and offered to join Mollie whenever his work schedule would allow it. Buster warmed up to John immediately. But, not quite the same way as he was with....

Mollie enjoyed spending time with John. Whether on their walks together or over dinner, he has shown a genuine interest in getting to know her. They have shared stories about their families, their childhoods, school, careers...everything. Mollie couldn't deny that she was attracted to him.

In time she told him about Brooke's baby. The look of concern and compassion in his eyes tugged at her heart. Although they had only known each other for a short time, Mollie felt he should know because she was literally "on call" for Brooke.

W

Weeks earlier, Brooke, Derek and Mollie created a plan for the baby's arrival. Brooke's specialists would all be on hand, outfits were purchased and packed and, because Brooke worried that a photographer might not be available if the delivery did not go as planned, Mollie volunteered to take these precious pictures for them. Everything was ready. All they could do now was wait and pray.

The three of them were spending a quiet Saturday together. Derek was working in the yard, Brooke and Buster were on the couch together watching a movie and Mollie was unpacking the remaining boxes from their move. She had just finished with the last box when Derek came in.

"I was thinking...we should go to church tomorrow," Brooke said matter-of-factly.

Derek and Mollie looked at each other.

"Honey, are you sure?" Derek asked as he walked over to the couch and sat next to Brooke.

"I'm sure. And...I'm sure you need a shower," she laughed as she gave him a kiss on the cheek.

"Gee, thanks," he chuckled as he got up to leave.

"Brooke, are you sure you want to go?" Mollie asked once she and Brooke were alone.

"Really, I am. I don't know why, but I just can't shake this feeling that we need to go; that I need to go," she said.

"Okay. Would you like me to call your parents and see if they would like to join us?" Mollie asked.

"That would be wonderful! Maybe they could come here in the morning and we could all ride together," Brooke suggested.

Mollie called her in-laws. She could hear the concern in their voices as they discussed plans for the next day. "They will be here at ten-thirty tomorrow," Mollie announced.

"Perfect!" Brooke replied.

The next morning, both Derek and Mollie asked Brooke if she was sure she wanted to venture out. She reassured them that she had not changed her mind. Mollie couldn't help but notice the constant smile on Brooke's face and a calm about her that Mollie hadn't seen in quite some time.

Brooke's parents arrived and they all rode to the church together in Derek's SUV. By the time they arrived, the sanctuary was already filling up. The only seats available to accommodate their large group were in the center of the room. Mollie worried about not being close to any of the aisles but Brooke seemed perfectly okay with sitting there.

After a time of worship through music, they all sat down, settling in for the message. But instead of the pastor beginning his sermon, he announced that they would be hearing from a guest speaker. Mollie didn't think much of it until the pastor introduced him. She immediately turned to Brooke.

"Did you know? Is this why you wanted to come?" Mollie whispered, feeling betrayed.

The look of absolute shock and confusion on Brooke's face gave Mollie her answer before Brooke even had a chance to speak. "I had no idea Mollie! I swear!" she whispered back.

Mollie wasn't ready for this, not yet. She wanted to get up and leave, but they were right in the middle of a row full of people. As much as she wanted to get out of there she didn't want to make a scene and she *definitely* didn't want him to see her. So, she folded her arms and glared at him; the man who took the love of her life away from her; the man who snuck into her heart.

Mollie could feel her body heat rising. The last thing she wanted to do was hear *his* side of the story. *Will he call it an accident? Will he have an excuse for his actions?* It was almost as if she could feel walls forming around her heart. *I will not let him trick me again. I will not feel for this man, not again, not ever.*

"Good morning. My name is Blake Williams and I am here today to share my testimony. But first, I would like to tell you about someone whom I admire and who has completely changed my life. Brett Walker was not only a man of honor but, more importantly, a man of God. He protected this great nation as a Marine. He encountered the unimaginable in Afghanistan only to return home to experience horrific flashbacks. We may be quick to ask why God would allow such things to happen. But the Bible reassures us that in all things God works for the good of those who love Him.[17] And that is just what God did. With God's help, Brett overcame those flashbacks and in the process met his wife, Mollie. Through his suffering, his faith was renewed and he found the love of his life.

"Because of God's work in his life, Brett planned to join the seminary once his time as a Marine was complete. He looked forward to a future of reaching others for Christ and starting a family with Mollie.

"Brett was a man of compassion, courage and character. You may be wondering why I am referring to him in the past tense. It is because I took the life of this incredible human being.

"It is a day I will never forget. I had just been fired from my dream job because of downsizing. I walked in on my girlfriend, who was going to move in with me and whom I planned to marry, cheating on me. I knew I would soon lose my apartment and brand-new sports car; things I had thought would make me feel happy and complete. I had officially hit rock bottom. I thought about calling my parents. They are devout Christians, but, at the time, I did not share their faith. They would often gently advise me to be practical, and I had been anything but in my decisions. I naturally assumed that my parents, and God, would judge me for my actions. That was the last thing I wanted so, instead of calling them, I decided to take matters into my own hands."

The walls Mollie put up before Blake spoke were instantly demolished when he began talking about Brett. A wave of emotions, and tears, overwhelmed her. As he spoke, memories of Brett flooded her mind and tore at her heart. *How does he know all of this? Did Brooke tell him our story?*

Her thoughts were interrupted when she realized he had stopped talking about Brett and was recounting that horrible day. The walls, and her anger, returned. Of course what Blake went through that day sounded awful but that was no excuse for getting behind the wheel drunk. As hard as she tried, Mollie couldn't stop herself from listening. Some part of her, deep down, really wanted to know more.

"I felt as if I had no one to turn to," he continued. "I wanted my pain and disappointment to go away. So, I drove to the nearest liquor store and asked the employee to point me in the direction of their strongest alcohol. I had been known to have a beer from time to time, but I was not very familiar with hard liquor. I grabbed a few bottles, paid and got into my car. My plan was to wait until I got to my apartment to start drinking. I would need all the liquid courage I could get to carry out my plan. You see, that day I had decided to end my life. I didn't want to continue living.

"As I sat in my car I felt my determination wavering. So, I thought that if I drank some of the alcohol right away that it would kick in right when I got to my apartment and I would be able to follow through with my plan. I was grossly naïve about how quickly this kind of alcohol would take effect. On my drive home, my car crossed over the center line and collided with an oncoming vehicle, killing the driver immediately," he said as tears streamed down his face.

Mollie tried to focus on the rest of Blake's testimony, but her brain couldn't move beyond the part when he mentioned his plan. Ever since Mollie read the police report she had wondered why someone would be drunk at that time of night. It was only eight o'clock when she and Brett had left the restaurant. Now it was all coming together in her mind.

Over the past few months, Mollie would get furious whenever someone referred to the crash as an accident. But she was beginning to realize that is *was* an accident. Blake didn't go out and get drunk with some buddies and then carelessly get behind the wheel. No, he was at his lowest and thought that alcohol would help him carry out his plan to end his life.

Mollie felt her body heaving as more puzzle pieces fell into place. Blake mentioned that he did not share the same faith as his parents, at least not at the time of the accident. If he *had* followed through with his plan, he would have spent eternity in Hell. Brett not only laid down his life for her but, in a way, laid it down for Blake too.

Instantly, Mollie remembered the times when Brooke would come home from her shift at the hospital with a look of despair in her eyes. Though she couldn't share details, she would talk of patients who had died and that she was unsure if they had a personal relationship with Jesus...if they were in Heaven. Mollie shuttered to think how devastated Blake's parents would have been if he had taken his life. Not only would they have grieved over his death, but they would have been left wondering where he would spend eternity.

Mollie looked up to see Blake steadying himself with the podium. He, too, was battling with his emotions. Instantly people stood up and began clapping. Mollie tried to stand but her legs wouldn't let her. *How I wish I had heard the rest of his testimony!* She tried to pull herself together before they got up to leave. Suddenly, she felt someone touch her hand.

"Would you like to talk with him?" Brooke asked. Her eyes were just as red and puffy as Mollie's.

"I don't know Brooke...I don't know if I am ready to..." That is when Mollie saw him out of the corner of her eye. There were several people around him. Mollie had hoped he wouldn't see her but the look on his face told her otherwise. He politely dismissed himself from the group and walked directly toward Mollie. She was frozen. She wanted to move, to leave, but she couldn't. She felt her body start to shake. *What am I going to say? What will he say?*

Brooke was the first to act. She greeted Blake and gave him a hug. Mollie could see the tears streaming down his face. "Derek, I think I need some water. Let's wait for Mollie in the lobby," Brooke said as she squeezed Mollie's hand and walked away.

Mollie was petrified. She didn't know what to say or do. She was about to open her mouth, hoping that something would come out, when suddenly she felt Blake's arms around her and heard him tell her over and over again how sorry he was. She wrapped her arms around him and felt the heat of tears once again on her cheeks. As they stepped back from their embrace, Mollie heard Derek shouting.

"Mollie! Hurry! Brooke's water just broke!"

Mollie sprinted to the doors, Blake right behind her. The look of panic on Derek and Brooke's faces sent chills through Mollie.

"Mollie, we have to get to the hospital right away. Could you go to the house and grab our bag? *Please hurry!*" Derek said as he tried to remain calm.

"Absolutely! Go!" Mollie ordered.

It wasn't until they were out of sight that Mollie realized that she did not have her car with her. Without thinking, she turned to Blake and asked if he could give her a ride. They ran to his car and she began giving him directions.

CHAPTER FORTY-ONE

Mollie almost didn't wait for the car to stop in front of the house before opening her door and sprinting inside to get the bag and her camera. As soon as she was back in the car they took off.

"Mollie, I know this is none of my business but Brooke and Derek seemed more scared than excited that the baby is coming. Is everything okay?"

In all the chaos Mollie had completely forgotten that Blake was not aware of the situation and how critical it was for them to get to the hospital as soon as possible.

"Brooke's baby girl has been diagnosed with Limb-body Wall Complex. Her internal abdominal organs have developed outside of her body. The doctors have told Brooke that if their baby is born alive, she will only live for a short time. And, they must deliver her by C-section because the baby will not likely survive a natural birth. Brooke was scheduled to have a C-section in a couple of weeks, but now that her water broke they have to get to the hospital right away."

Lord, please be with Brooke. Please let her have time with her baby girl before You take her to Heaven. And please get us there in time so that I can take pictures of this precious angel while she is here on Earth.

Blake pulled up to the hospital entrance and Mollie raced inside. She frantically asked for directions to the labor and delivery ward. One of the nurses quickly got her into scrubs and ready to join them in the operating room. There were doctors and nurses everywhere. Mollie immediately walked up to Brooke as she lay on the operating table.

"Oh Mollie! I'm so glad you made it!" Brooke said as tears streamed down the sides of her face.

Mollie bent down and gave Brooke a hug. She was about to say something when she heard one of the doctors ask for a scalpel. Immediately, Mollie's attention turned to the other side of the curtain. Carefully and quickly, the doctors worked together, and soon the baby was out and rushed over to a warming bed. Mollie followed right behind snapping picture after picture. There was even a brief moment when her beautiful blue eyes were open. *Oh Lord, does this mean there is a chance?*

One of the specialists came over to examine her. The look on his face confirmed the prognosis. Even though their precious daughter was alive, it would not be for long. A nurse gently wrapped her in a pink blanket and brought her to Derek. He held her close to Brooke's face. Brooke whispered to her as she placed her finger inside her daughter's delicate hand and gently kissed her cheek. It was the most beautiful and heartbreaking moment Mollie had ever witnessed. Only by God's grace was she able to keep her hands, and her emotions, steady to capture these precious memories.

One of the nurses walked up to Derek and asked if they had a name for their little girl.

"Darlene Grace," he replied, barely above a whisper.

"What a beautiful name," the nurse said as she gently placed her hand on his shoulder.

As soon as the doctors were finished, Brooke was taken to a private recovery room. Her parents joined them and told Derek that his parents were on their way. They prayed that his parents would get to see their granddaughter before her time on Earth was through.

God heard their prayers. An hour later, Derek's parents walked into the recovery room, and within minutes of their arrival Darlene's color began to change. Their little girl had been called back to Heaven. Although there was sadness there was also peace.

Some would say that God did not perform a miracle that day, but they would be wrong. In fact, He performed many miracles.

Not only did God get them to the hospital in time to still have a C-section, but He also had *all* of Brooke's specialists working at the hospital that day and on hand for the delivery. And, only by the grace of God did Mollie make it to the operating room just minutes before Darlene's birth.

After the delivery, the doctors informed Brooke that the umbilical cord had been extremely short. It is related to Darlene's condition and meant that a natural birth would not only have been fatal for Darlene but also extremely dangerous for Brooke. Placental abruption could have also occurred, not only during a natural birth but even during the pregnancy. God had protected Brooke from harm and gave them two whole hours with Darlene before she was carried up to Heaven. All of this was undeniable evidence of God's presence and love.

They spent the next two hours holding Darlene and recounting God's many blessings. When the nurse came in she looked at the name tag on the bassinet. "What a beautiful name," she said as she gently gathered Darlene in her arms.

"It means tenderly loved blessing," Brooke replied, struggling to speak.

The nurse's eyes glistened as she smiled at the delicate child in her arms.

As Mollie took pictures of the nurse with Darlene in her arms, she envisioned Brett cradling his new niece, showing her all the wonder and beauty that now surrounds her. Darlene's short life may leave a hole in their hearts, but they know that she has now been made whole. And, she is not alone. She has her uncle to watch over her. Mollie walked over to Brooke's bed and sat beside her.

"Brett is watching over her, I just know it," Mollie whispered and wrapped her arms around Brooke.

Mollie could tell that Brooke was exhausted, emotionally and physically. They all were. Brooke and Derek needed some time to be together, alone.

As Mollie and the others walked down the hallway, Derek's father offered to give them all a ride back to the house. They were just about to the elevators when Mollie saw him. *He's still here?* She politely excused herself from the group and told them that she would find her own way home.

Even though his back was to her, Mollie knew it was Blake. He was slouched over in his chair. *Is he asleep?* As Mollie got closer she realized he wasn't sleeping, he was praying. She gently placed her hand on his shoulder and he immediately looked up.

His eyes were bloodshot and his cheeks were stained. Mollie felt her own eyes well up with tears.

"Is she...is she gone?" he asked.

Mollie nodded her head.

He stood up and put his arms around her. In the warmth of Blake's embrace, Mollie let her emotions have their way with her. "I'm so sorry," he cried over and over again. Mollie couldn't speak. All she could do was hold on to him.

Blake's mind was racing as they walked in silence to his car. *What do I say? How can I help her?* Blake suggested stopping for something to eat but Mollie said she was too tired.

"May I at least stop on the way and get you something?" he offered. "You haven't eaten since this morning."

"That would be nice. Thank you," she said, staring straight ahead.

The moment Blake had been dreading finally came as he pulled into the driveway. *What do I say when she gets out of the car? Will I ever see her again? Lord, please help me!* Instead of opening her door, Mollie sat there, still staring straight ahead. *Please Lord, show me what to do!* Suddenly, without thinking, Blake placed his hand on hers.

"I'll be praying for you, all of you."

Blake thought she would pull her hand away but, instead, she turned and looked at him. The only time he has ever seen someone in that much pain was when he looked into the eyes of his mother after his sentencing. He wanted to gather Mollie up in his arms and never let go.

"Thank you. Please pray especially for Brooke. I think the worst lies just ahead," she said.

The look on Blake's face must have shown his confusion.

"I thought the hardest part was going to be before Darlene's birth, the waiting and the worrying. But now, even though we know she is in Heaven, an emptiness remains, especially for Brooke. Please pray that God will show me how to help her," Mollie said as tears began gathering in her eyes.

"I will. I promise," Blake whispered as he gently squeezed her hand.

"Thank you. I...I have to go," she stammered and got out of the car.

Before driving off, Blake quickly dialed Ruby. She was the only person he could think of who might be able to help Brooke...who understood this kind of loss...

Over the next few days, Brooke continued to recover from her surgery as funeral plans were made. Darlene would be wrapped up in a pastel blanket Brooke had crocheted and wear a beautiful christening dress that had been purchased months ago. While Brooke was still in the hospital, Mollie brought her two matching cross necklaces, one much smaller than the other. One was for Darlene to wear and the other for Brooke.

"Oh Mollie, they are beautiful! Thank you," she cried and wrapped her arms around her. "And, thank you for taking pictures of Darlene's birth. We have only looked at a few of them, but the first ones took our breath away. We didn't even know she had her eyes open when she was first born. We will cherish those pictures forever. Thank you!" she sobbed.

Mollie hated seeing Brooke in such pain. She felt so helpless. She stepped out into the hallway and immediately dialed Ruby's number.

"Hi Sweetie," Ruby answered. Mollie could tell by the tone in her voice that she already knew. Blake must have told her.

"Hi Ruby. Did Blake tell you?"

"Yes, he did. We are praying for you hon! If there is anything I can do to help…"

"Oh Ruby! I don't know what to do! Losing Brett was the most painful thing I have ever gone through but to lose a child…I cannot even imagine what she is going through. I was wondering if you would still be willing to meet with Brooke. I know that there is never truly an end to the grieving process but maybe, if she sees how you and James have worked through it, she will regain some hope for the future."

"Of course, Sugar. You just let me know when she is ready and I'll be there," Ruby said with such tenderness in her voice.

"Thank you Ruby! I will. I'll call you later."

Mollie had thought about having Brooke and Ruby meet before Darlene's birth, but she wondered if it would put too much focus on loss, on death. Their attention needed to be on the *life* that was growing inside Brooke. But now, Mollie knew without a doubt that Brooke would need someone to talk to, someone who understood. Perhaps after the funeral she will be ready.

CHAPTER FORTY-TWO

As hard as he tried, Blake couldn't keep Mollie off of his mind. Knowing that she was hurting and he wasn't there to help her, to be with her, was eating away at him. *Who am I kidding? I'm probably the last person she wants near her. Perhaps she has forgiven me and is at least able to tolerate being around me but...to love me? Impossible.*

Why can't I just move on? I can tell that Sara is interested in me. She is an amazing woman so why am I still longing for someone I can never have? Lord, please help me!

Blake tried his best to hide his emotions, especially at work, but he knew that Sara could tell that something was wrong.

"Blake, is everything okay? You haven't been yourself lately," she asked as they took Cookie and Sam for a walk.

"I'm sorry. I guess I just have a lot on my mind," he said, as he stared at the ground.

"Well, if you ever want to talk about it, I'm here," she said as she placed her hand on his shoulder.

Blake looked at her hand and then at her. "Thanks."

Then, without even thinking it through, he began telling her everything. He told Sara about that horrible day, the accident, Mollie, Brooke, Darlene...everything. Then, he waited. He waited for her excuse, some reason why she suddenly needed to leave and then never see her again.

Instead, she just kept walking. Blake didn't know if she was waiting to see if there was more or if she was trying to process all that he had just told her. He walked beside her, unsure of what to say.

Suddenly, she stopped and turned toward Blake, looking deep into his eyes. "Blake, now I understand why you have been so guarded. You were afraid to tell me about the accident, afraid that I would judge you. But I care about you, Blake. I think you know that by now. Every one of us has a past riddled with mistakes. What matters is whether we learn from them. I know without a doubt that you have. What matters to me is your future, and I was hoping to be a part of it. But, I now know that your heart is spoken for. I'll be praying for you," she said, desperately fighting back tears.

"I'm so sorry. It doesn't make sense..."

"Love rarely does," she added. "All I know is that you have to see this through. Otherwise, you will spend the rest of your life wondering, 'What if...' Who knows what the future holds."

"Only God does."

"Exactly," she said, her lips quivering as she smiled. She gently kissed Blake on the cheek as she placed Cookie's leash in his hand and then walked to her car. As she drove off, Blake wondered if he would ever see her again. Only God knows the answer to that question...

W

Any time Mollie wasn't helping with the funeral plans she was praying for Brooke. She knew that Brooke wouldn't be able to get through the funeral without God's help. So instead of focusing on their sorrow, Darlene's funeral was a celebration of her life and the hope of Heaven. *One day we will be together again. I just wish it didn't feel like a lifetime away.*

The one thing Mollie didn't foresee was how Darlene's funeral would rekindle all of her loneliness and pain from losing Brett. How she would have given anything to have him with her, to hold her and tell her that everything will be okay. As she watched Brooke and Derek together she no longer felt the sting of jealousy. Instead, she thanked God that they had each other, especially now.

Thank you Lord for providing Brooke with so many amazing friends and family to help her through this. Although we don't understand it, may Darlene's short life bring You glory and honor.

John had offered to come with Mollie to the funeral but she felt that she should devote all of her attention to Brooke and her needs. He understood completely. Mollie promised to call him when things settled down. The truth was, she was avoiding him.

She couldn't explain it. Any woman would be thrilled to find someone like John. He's compassionate, respectful, brave, strong, handsome, and the list goes on and on. In her head, he is the perfect guy, but somehow her heart hasn't gotten the message. It didn't make sense. She knew that she still wasn't ready to give her heart completely to someone, but she thought she would at least have *some* romantic feelings toward him by now. *Maybe it is just too soon and we need to spend more time together. Or, maybe I am forcing something that just isn't there because I don't want to be alone. Or, maybe, my heart is already spoken for... Lord, this doesn't make sense!*

A week went by after the funeral and Mollie knew it was time to call John. Her prayer was that he would understand and be willing to give her some time, some space. If they were meant to be together then God would make it happen.

As much as Mollie wanted to tell him over the phone, she forced herself do it in person. They met for lunch and she was so nervous that she couldn't eat.

"Mollie, is everything okay?"

"I...I'm so sorry," she stammered, trying not to cry.

"Sorry?"

"John, I can't explain it. You're so wonderful. Maybe I just need more time," she blurted out.

Mollie tried to look at him but it was impossible. As she reached for a napkin to dry her eyes, she felt his hand on hers.

"Mollie, it's okay. You have been through so much. I care about you deeply. But, if you need some time, some space, that's okay."

His words unleashed a torrent of tears from within her. *What am I doing? Why am I pushing someone like him away?* The thoughts in her head were screaming at her to undo what she had just put into motion. But, her heart...her heart stayed the course. *Lord, is this really Your will? Am I not supposed to be with John? This doesn't make sense!* Suddenly, Mollie felt a warmth come over her and the words of Proverbs quieted her thoughts, "Trust in the Lord with all your heart and lean not on your own understanding.[3]"

Mollie took a few deep breaths and looked into John's eyes. *He deserves to know the truth...all of it.* Suddenly, she began telling him everything; about meeting Steven at the shelter, how she developed feelings for him, adopting Buster, discovering that Steven was really Blake, hearing his testimony...everything.

John sat there for a moment. Mollie searched his eyes, wondering what he was thinking. The look on his face was almost too much to bear.

"Mollie, as much as I care about you and want to be with you, I don't want part of you. I guess I'm a little selfish that way. You have been fighting these feelings for Blake and they haven't gone away. Maybe, like you said, your heart was very vulnerable when you met him. Whatever the reason, you need time to figure this out," he said, his eyes glistening.

"Oh John, I am so sorry! None of this makes sense. I feel like I am making a terrible mistake!"

"None of us is ever one hundred percent sure we are doing the right thing. That is where trust and prayer come in. Mollie, I'll be praying for you, all of you. God will show us who we are meant to be with. We just have to be patient," he added as he gently kissed her hand.

As Mollie drove home she felt as if she was going to be sick. *Oh Lord, if I have made a mistake please fix it! I don't know what to do!*

Mollie was thankful to find Brooke and Buster napping on the couch as she entered the living room. She too needed some rest and a chance to quiet her thoughts.

174

When Mollie awoke, she found Brooke working at the dining room table. Over the past week, they had been diligently working on a scrapbook of Darlene's life. The pictures that were taken during the pregnancy were especially difficult for Brooke to look at. She would place her hands on her now empty womb and long to feel Darlene's kicks, her signs of life. Brooke admitted that there have been times when she has been angry that her water broke and she didn't get to have more time with Darlene. She knew that this was only one of many feelings she would wrestle with for the rest of her life. It would be easy to let her anger overshadow the fact that she got to hold her little angel for two glorious hours before she left this world.

The scrapbook was filled with pictures and Scripture. God's Word, written thousands of years ago, applied so clearly, so beautifully, to what they were going through today.

During Darlene's birth, and the four hours they had with her, Mollie had taken over one thousand pictures. She feared that having that many pictures would be overwhelming, especially for Brooke. But she didn't want Brooke and Derek to miss any moments, like the brief time that Darlene had her eyes open. As Mollie and Brooke sat together, side by side, looking at the last of the pictures, Brooke suddenly stopped and looked at Mollie.

"Mollie, are you okay?" she asked, searching Mollie's eyes.

Mollie didn't want to tell her. Brooke already had so much on her mind. Mollie opened her mouth to tell Brooke that she was fine, but instead, she began telling Brooke about her conversation with John.

"Brooke, I'm so sorry! I shouldn't be bothering you with this," Mollie said tearfully.

"Oh Mollie, please don't think that! You know, I have also been thinking about Blake a lot lately. What he said at the end of his testimony has been replaying in my mind."

The last thing Mollie remembered Blake talking about was the accident. She had been so overwhelmed with emotions that she didn't hear the rest.

"I...I only remember him talking about the accident. After that, I was..."

"Mollie, you need to hear it, all of it," Brooke said matter-of-factly.

The way Brooke said it, so clearly, so confidently, reminded Mollie of the night before Darlene's birth. Even with all of them questioning Brooke, she stood firm when she said she wanted to go to church. And then... *Could it be? Lord, were you working through her that day? Are you now?*

"*Trust in the Lord with all your heart and lean not on your own understanding.³*" Those words in Proverbs once again echoed in Mollie's mind. She knew what she needed to do...

W

When Ruby saw Mollie's name appear on her phone she answered immediately.

"Hi Sugar! How are you?" Ruby asked eagerly.

"Hi Ruby. I'm okay," Mollie replied and Ruby could tell that something was wrong.

"Honey, what is it?"

Suddenly, Mollie began pouring her heart out. She told Ruby about John and the conversation they had. Ruby could tell that Mollie was questioning her feelings for Blake and wondering if she had made a mistake by letting John go. She was about to tell Mollie about Blake and the conversation *he* had with Sara. But, something held her back. Instead, Ruby listened and prayed for her dear friend.

"Ruby, I need your help."

"Anything, Sugar. Just tell me what to do."

"Could you find out where Blake will be speaking next? But, *please* do not let him know that you are asking for me!" she begged.

"Of course. But, I'm confused. I thought you already heard his testimony."

"I did. But, I got so emotional that I didn't hear much after he talked about the accident. Brooke says I need to hear it," Mollie explained.

"You do Sugar! I'll find out and get back to you."

"Thank you Ruby! Oh, I was wondering when you might be free to come over to the house. Brooke said she would love to meet you."

"I have Sunday off. Maybe I could come by in the afternoon, around two o'clock?" Ruby suggested.

"That would be wonderful! I will double check with Brooke but we should be available. I'll let you know. Thanks again Ruby...for everything!" Mollie said as she hung up the phone.

Ruby knew exactly how she was going to find out where Blake would be speaking next. Now she just needed to wait for the right opportunity.

CHAPTER FORTY-THREE

"I just got off the phone with Ruby. She would love to stop by on Sunday afternoon. Would two o'clock be okay?" Mollie asked, hoping that Brooke and Derek did not already have plans.

"That would be wonderful! I can't wait to meet her," Brooke replied excitedly.

"Brooke, there is something about Ruby I haven't told you and I think you should know this before she comes on Sunday. Not only do I want you to meet her because she has become a dear friend of mine but because I think she may be able to help you."

"Help me?"

"Yes. You see, Ruby and her husband lost their son when he was four months old."

"Oh," Brooke said as fresh tears gathered in her eyes.

"Brooke, if this is too much I can call her right now and…"

"Mollie, it's okay. God places people in our lives to help us. And the truth is, I need help. I am trying to stay strong and focus on the blessings but there are times when I want to slip into a place of anger and grief. As painful as it might be, for the both of us, I want to meet her, to talk with her," she said as tears quietly streamed down her face.

Mollie wrapped her arms around Brooke and rocked her as she cried. Mollie never seemed to know what to say. All she could offer Brooke was a shoulder to cry on.

"I think I might take Buster for a walk. Are you feeling up to joining us?" Mollie asked.

"Maybe a short walk. My recovery from the C-section has been slower than I anticipated. Hopefully some fresh air and a *little* exercise will do me some good."

After their walk, Brooke went to her room to rest. Buster was right behind her. Mollie smiled as she watched them. *My dog may be a mutt but he has a heart of gold.*

Mollie was about to call Ruby when her phone started ringing. She was surprised to see Ruby's name appear on her screen.

"Hi! I was just about to call you," Mollie said.

"Well, perfect timing then," she replied and Mollie could tell she was smiling by the tone of her voice.

"I talked to Brooke and she would love for you to come over on Sunday."

"Wonderful! And, I have some news for you!" Her words made Mollie's stomach instantly tie into knots.

"Oh?" Mollie asked, trying to mask her nervousness.

"Blake will be speaking at Covenant Church this weekend. The first service is Saturday night at five o'clock. There are other services too if that one won't work for you."

"He told you all of this?" Mollie asked, suddenly afraid that somehow Blake would figure out that Ruby was getting this information for her.

"Not exactly. I decided to find out in a round-about way," Ruby said.

"A round-about way?"

"You see, a few weeks ago, Blake mentioned that he has a speaking engagement every Sunday until the end of the year. So today, I pretended to forget and asked him if he would like to go to church on Sunday with James and me. He thanked me for the offer but said he would not be able to go because he was speaking at Covenant Church all weekend. I was a bit confused when he said, 'all weekend.' He then explained that they have a Saturday night service and two Sunday services. I told him that I was worried about him having to tell his story that many times. He assured me that they already have a plan in place if it proves to be too much for him. They are going to tape the first service and, if necessary, replay it for the other services. And, I can assure *you* that he has no idea that I was asking for you," she said. Mollie could hear the excitement in Ruby's voice.

"Thank you Ruby!"

"Of course, Sugar. So, I'll see you on Sunday at two?"

"Yes! I can't wait to see you," Mollie added as she hung up the phone.

Saturday was still two days away but Mollie's stomach was already full of butterflies. She tried to keep herself busy, but by Saturday afternoon she was a wreck. *Maybe I should wait and go tomorrow.*

Mollie heard a knock on her bedroom door.

"Mollie, may I come in?" Brooke asked kindly.

"Of course."

"Are you okay?" Brooke asked as she sat down.

"Yes...no...I don't know."

She placed her arm around Mollie's shoulders. "Would you like me to go with you?"

"Thanks for the offer but I think this is something that I need to do on my own," Mollie replied, startled by her own words.

"Okay. We will be praying for you," she said as she gave Mollie a hug.

"Thanks!" Mollie replied. "I'll need it!"

Mollie's body began to shake as she drove to the church. The sanctuary was almost full by the time she walked in. She found a spot toward the back near one of the doors. She wanted to make sure she could slip out as soon as the service was over. She promised Brooke that she would listen to Blake's testimony. She didn't say she would talk to him.

By the time the pastor introduced Blake, Mollie's entire body was shaking. She felt the sting of fresh tears as he once again talked about Brett and the accident. *Lord, please give me the strength to get through this. I need to hear it all.*

Emotion filled Blake's voice as he continued. "So often people use the phrase, 'Everything happens for a reason.' I tried to apply that to my situation and it only made me angry. I questioned God over and over again. Why wasn't I the one to die? I welcomed death and Brett had so much to live for. The answer was simple and yet it took me months before I could truly embrace it. The reason God spared my life is because of His immense love for me.

"God knew that if I had died that night that my final destination would have been Hell. Brett had a personal relationship with Jesus. His friends and family can rest in the peace of knowing that he is in Heaven. If I had died, my parents would have spent the rest of their lives wondering, and worrying, about where I would spend eternity.

"And even though I was beginning to understand God's love, I was riddled with guilt. Thoughts of suicide still plagued me. I felt so ashamed of what I had done and the hurt and pain I saw in the eyes of Brett's family was worse than anything I could have imagined.

"I began believing that if I took my life that it would bring his family a sense of justice, of closure. These dark thoughts started to consume me.

"I have clung to the words in Jeremiah 29:11 about how God has plans for me to prosper and to give me hope and a future.[25] But I didn't feel like I deserved a future, not after what I had done. Then a friend shared with me that the prophet Jeremiah said these words to the Israelites after being exiled because they had turned from God and done terrible things. God hadn't given up on them, and He hasn't given up on me. It was then that I realized that if I took my life I would be dishonoring Brett, and more importantly, dishonoring God.

"Every morning is still a struggle, every day a battle field. The devil is constantly whispering to me, trying to lure me to those dark places. I realized that I have to, 'Put on the full armor of God, so that (I) can take (my) stand against the devil's schemes.[46] Only with God's help can I win this battle. He continues to strengthen and encourage me through His Word and the people He has placed in my life.

"I have been given a second chance, and I will spend the rest of my life serving God and honoring Him, and Brett. My prayer is that others will learn from my mistakes and not wait to start a personal relationship with Jesus. And one day, when my time has come, I pray that Jesus, and Brett, will greet me and say, 'Well done, good and faithful servant.[38]' Thank you."

Immediately, people rose to their feet and applause rang out. Mollie sat there, unable to move, her head buried in her hands. As painful as Brett's death has been she could not imagine what it must be like to carry the guilt of taking someone's life. *What if my words, my actions had driven him to...? Oh Lord, thank You for protecting him! Thank You he's alive!*

Mollie's body ached as she walked out of the church. She wanted to talk to Blake but not yet, not here. She needed to get home and rest.

Brooke waited anxiously for Mollie to get back from church. Ever since Darlene's birth, Blake's words have been running through Brooke's mind. When the doctors told them about the umbilical cord being extremely short and how that could have harmed Brooke, she started asking God, "Why? Why didn't you take me too?"

Brooke has found herself in the dark places Blake talked about. Thoughts of emptiness, grief, anger and depression would envelope her. If it weren't for the Scripture journal Mollie gave her and the amazing people God has placed in her life, Brooke didn't know what she would do.

God could have taken Brooke to Heaven with Darlene, but He spared her life because she has work here on Earth left to do. So, instead of asking God, "Why?" Brooke has started asking, "How?" *How can I serve You Lord? Please show me. I want to glorify You through our loss. I too want to hear, "Well done, good and faithful servant,[38]" when I see You, and Darlene, one day.*

Brooke's thoughts were interrupted when she heard the front door open. She could tell the moment Mollie walked in that she had been crying. Brooke wasn't sure what to say. *Does she want to talk about it? Please Lord, show me what to do!*

"Hi," Brooke said as she walked to the entryway.

"Hi," Mollie sniffled.

"Dinner is just about ready. Hungry?" Brooke asked, trying to keep the conversation light.

"Not really. I think I am just going to go to bed," Mollie said, barely above a whisper.

"Okay," Brooke replied, gently touching her arm. "Derek and I are planning to go to church in the morning. Maybe we could meet up for lunch afterwards?" she suggested.

"Sure. Thanks."

Mollie remained in her room all night. By the time Derek and Brooke were ready to leave for church the next morning, Mollie was still in her bedroom. Brooke didn't think that listening to Blake's testimony again would completely shut Mollie down like this. *Oh Lord, did I make a mistake? I feel like she has regressed instead of moving forward. Please Lord, show me what to do!*

After church Brooke called to invite Mollie to lunch but she politely declined. *Lord, I don't know what is going on. Please help me help her!*

The moment Brooke and Derek got home she called out for Mollie. There was no answer. That is when she saw a note on the kitchen table.

Buster and I went for a walk. Be back soon.

Brooke waited for what seemed like hours and breathed a sigh of relief when she saw Mollie and Buster walking toward the house.

"Mollie, is everything okay?" Brooke blurted out as soon as they walked in.

"Oh Brooke, I'm so sorry if I worried you! I just needed some time to think, and pray. Blake's words opened my eyes. I have been dishonoring God, and Brett, by harboring this anger and unforgiveness. And Blake? His pain and guilt are so deep and all I have done is add to it. I keep thanking God that he didn't take his life. God has shown me over and over again that He is with me and that He has a plan for everything if I would just trust Him. And now

I think He has shown me a glimpse of His plan. I'll tell you and Ruby about it when she gets here."

CHAPTER FORTY-FOUR

A nervous energy was building inside Brooke. She didn't know what she was more excited for, Ruby's visit or Mollie's announcement. From the moment Ruby arrived, Brooke felt a connection to her. Ruby hugged Brooke as if they had known each other their whole lives and her eyes danced as they looked at Darlene's baby book. You would never know that she, too, has lost a child.

As they sat together in the living room, Ruby shared memories of Junior. Brooke's tears came quietly as Ruby talked about his big brown eyes, his cheeks that begged to be pinched, his smile that could light up a room and his laugh that still echoes in her heart. Then she pulled out a piece of paper and began telling Brooke about that day; the day when Junior went to Heaven and she felt she was in Hell. Brooke's body began to heave as Ruby recounted the events and the emotions that raged within her.

It was as if Ruby was reading Brooke's mind, like she was looking in a mirror.

"There were so many moments when I would become depressed and angry over all the things Junior would miss out on; his first steps, his first day of school, his first love, his...life. I felt a bitterness taking root within me. But, thankfully, God placed an incredible counselor in my life.

"My counselor read from Philippians when Paul wrote that for him, 'living means living for Christ, and dying is even better.[47]' I realized that even though Junior would not experience many milestones in this world, he was already spending eternity with our Heavenly Father. There is nothing in this world that can compare to that.

"Paul said that if he lives, he can do more fruitful work for Christ.[48] I realized that even though I was alive, I wasn't living and I definitely was not living for Christ, at least not fully. It was then that James and I decided that we would share our story, no matter how difficult it might be, to bring glory to God and to honor Junior. In 2 Corinthians it says, '(God) comforts us in all our troubles so that we can comfort others.[35]' We realized that there is purpose in our pain and that when someone who is going through a similar situation hears our story, they know that they are not alone. James and I recently joined a support group for people who have lost young children because we also need to know that we are not alone.

"Brooke, God wants you to know that you are not alone. He is always there for you, and so am I," Ruby added, her eyes glistening.

Brooke threw her arms around Ruby. Her words had lifted a weight off of Brooke's shoulders. God sent her an angel that day. He knew that Brooke needed someone to talk to, someone who understood the thoughts and feelings that were suffocating her.

"Thank you, Ruby," Brooke whispered. "You are an answer to my prayers."

As Mollie watched Ruby and Brooke together she knew, without a doubt, that God had placed them in each other's lives for a reason, and that reason is because He loves them. *When we care for others and love them as Christ loves us we get glimpses of Heaven.*

Mollie's thoughts were suddenly interrupted when she heard Brooke say her name.

"So Mollie, are you ready to tell us your plan?" Brooke asked eagerly.

"Oh. Of course. I didn't want to interrupt..."

"Oh, Sugar, don't you worry. I have a feeling the three of us will be spending a lot of time together," Ruby said as she squeezed Brooke's hand. "Now, what's this about a plan?"

"Well...last night I went to Covenant Church to listen to Blake's testimony. I...I didn't realize that he still had thoughts of taking his life, even after the accident. It never crossed my mind that my actions, and my words, might drive him to..." she paused, trying to suppress her emotions. "It reminded me of something you told me Ruby, that our tongues can bring life or death. In that moment I thanked God that Blake is alive. I never thought I would be thanking God for that.

"And Ruby, ever since you shared your testimony with me I have noticed that your words immediately speak to me when I face difficult moments. The Scripture, songs and advice you have shared with me have been my anchor in the storm. It's like you just said, when we share with others they realize that they are not alone, that there is someone out there who understands. And when you and James give your testimonies together, you not only speak of regret, guilt and pain, you also tell about the power of love and forgiveness. All of us can relate. Each of has had moments when we have been hurt or been the one to do the hurting. I think that is why your message is so powerful.

"I don't want to continue dishonoring God, and Brett, by harboring this anger. Blake wasn't the only one God saved that night. He could have taken me to Heaven with Brett. Instead, I am here and, to me, that means that I still have work to do. I haven't been doing that and, last night, I asked God to show me His plan; that I was giving Him control of my life.

"When I awoke this morning, my mind was racing. All these verses and thoughts were running through my head. I found some paper and began writing them down. It was as if I could not write fast enough. When I was finished, I sat back and read my notes. It was then that I realized what I had just done...I had written my testimony. And I knew why. God wants me to share my story, and He wants me to give my testimony...with Blake."

A look of shock came over both Brooke and Ruby. Then slowly, almost simultaneously, a smile crept across each of their faces.

"Oh, Sugar! We are so proud of you," Ruby exclaimed as she walked over and gave Mollie a hug. Brooke followed right behind her.

"Well, I still need to talk to Blake about this..."

"Oh, Sugar! I just know he'll be thrilled!"

"Is he working tomorrow? I was thinking about stopping by the shelter to talk with him," Mollie said, suddenly feeling nervous.

"Yes, he is working tomorrow. Why don't you come by in the morning? Should I tell him your coming?" Ruby asked with a light in her eyes.

"Let's not. I was thinking of surprising him by bringing Buster along," Mollie replied.

"My lips are sealed, Sugar. How about you stop by around ten o'clock? He'll just be finishing up feeding the animals," she said. Mollie could hear the excitement in her voice.

W

The next morning Mollie was a nervous wreck as she drove to the shelter. *Oh Lord, I don't think I can do this. Maybe I should wait. Maybe this is too soon.*

Mollie was jolted from her thoughts by the sound of Buster barking and pacing in the back seat. As soon as she let him out of the car he bolted for the front doors. *Even after all these months he hasn't forgotten about...*

Mollie's nervousness must have been obvious because as soon as she walked in Ruby gave her a big hug and whispered, "You can do this, Sugar. God is with you."

She wiped the tears from her eyes. *Pull yourself together, Mollie. You can't start crying now.*

Mollie heard Ruby page Blake. Her knees felt weak and her stomach ached. She began breathing deeply when, suddenly, she felt the leash rip from her hands. She watched as Buster ran to Blake, knocking him over and covering him with kisses. Seeing them together and hearing Blake's laughter brought Mollie to tears.

She dug in her purse for some Kleenex, and when she looked up Blake was right in front of her. The way he looked into her eyes filled her with such warmth that she knew she was blushing.

"Hi," she said sheepishly.

"Hi," he replied with a tenderness that reached every part of her.

"We...I...I thought you might like some visitors," Mollie stammered.

"Thank you for thinking of me."

Buster was tugging on his leash, begging to go outside. Blake turned to Mollie and smiled. "I think someone wants to go for a walk. Shall we join him?"

They walked out the front doors and toward the dirt road. All the things Mollie planned to say were gone. Her mind was a complete blank. *Oh Lord, help me! I don't know what to say!*

"How are Brooke and Derek?" Blake asked, a sadness in his voice.

"They are taking one day at a time. Ruby came by yesterday, and I can already tell what a difference it has made in Brooke. I thank God every day that Ruby is in my life. She has been an answer to prayer, for me and for Brooke."

"Me too. There are days when I still cannot believe what she and James have been through. It would have been so easy for them to keep it to themselves but their willingness to share their story played a huge part in my faith journey. My hope and prayer is that God will use my story to help others and let them know that they are not alone." Mollie could see tears gathering in his eyes.

"I heard you speak at Covenant Church on Saturday night," she admitted nervously.

"You did?"

"Mmmm, hmmm. I had gotten quite emotional the first time I heard you speak and didn't hear the end of your testimony. Brooke told me I needed to hear it again, all of it."

"How did you...Ruby!" he exclaimed. "Oh, how I love that gal!"

"She is pretty clever, I must say," Mollie added, smiling.

"That she is. I wish I would have known you were there," he said. Even though she was looking down at the ground, Mollie could tell that Blake was looking at her.

"I'm sorry," she said, unable to fight back the tears.

Blake placed his hand on Mollie's arm. "Mollie, it's okay. I didn't mean to upset you."

"No, it's not that. I mean, I *am* sorry I didn't tell you that I was going to be there. But...what I meant was...I'm sorry...for everything. The way I treated you, the things I have said. I'm so sorry," she sobbed.

Suddenly she felt Blake's arms around her. He gently stroked her hair and whispered, "I understand. It's okay. It's okay."

"You...you...wanted to end your life. I know that I hurt you. I'm so sorry if I was part of the reason you wanted to..."

"Mollie, you were the sliver of light in my darkness," he said, his voice full of emotion. "I'm so sorry for hurting you. I never meant to hurt anyone. I hope you can find it in your heart to forgive me," he sobbed.

"I already have," Mollie whispered and she felt Blake's whole body begin to shake.

Blake felt a warmth and peace come over him that he had never experienced before. He wanted to stay in that moment forever. Mollie stepped back and looked deep into his eyes.

"There's something I want to show you," she said as she wiped the tears from her eyes.

She reached into her purse and pulled out an envelope. Blake's heart was racing as she handed it to him.

"I understand if you can't read it now. You need to get back to..."

"I'll stay late. This is important," he interrupted. They began to walk back to the shelter.

As they sat down in the empty conference room, Blake gently opened the envelope. He tried to steady his hands but it was impossible. He looked over at Mollie. She was looking down at Buster as she petted him. Blake could tell she was nervous too.

The night of the accident changed my life. When my father told me that Brett was dead I was overwhelmed with a pain that I had never experienced before. Anger, grief, depression and guilt consumed me. How could this have happened?

I instantly felt hatred toward the man who took Brett's life and vowed never to forgive him. Jesus tells us to love our enemies but I tried to rationalize why that didn't apply to me. In my mind, he didn't deserve forgiveness.

Over the next several months there were times when I felt close to God, times I wondered where God was, and times I pushed Him away. A war was raging within me. I felt like I was being consumed by my feelings of anger and betrayal. It wasn't until I read 1 Peter 5:8 that I began to understand why. The Bible tells us that Satan prowls around like a roaring lion, looking for someone to devour.[49] *I've come to the conclusion that he tries to accomplish this in one of two ways, or sometimes both. I call them his Slay and Sway methods of attack.*

Slay refers to those moments that rock your world and shake your faith; those times when Satan tries to devour you whole. It might be a devastating diagnosis, betrayal, addiction, a tragedy...something so big, so overwhelming, that you wonder where God is in all of it; something that makes you doubt God...question Him. Losing Brett was Satan's Slay in my life. I felt as if my world had come to an end and I had been cut to the core.

I tried to move forward. I turned to God's Word and was surrounded by amazing friends and family. That is when Satan unleashed the Sway. The Sway is when Satan whispers lies that plant seeds of doubt in your faith in God. It can be so subtle that you don't even realize what is happening. It is Satan's way of devouring you piece-by-piece.

Satan preyed on my weakened faith and made me feel justified in my anger. He kept my focus on what I couldn't have, a future with Brett. I continued to listen to Satan's lies that I was better off on my own, that I didn't need God or anyone else. I even felt a false sense of peace. I didn't realize that my pride was keeping me from the people I needed the most and who needed me the most. I had been so caught up in my pain that I failed to see how my words, and my actions, were affecting those around me, especially Blake.

Thankfully, God never stopped pursuing me. He continued to put people and events in my life to draw me back to Him. He helped me restore my relationships and opened my eyes.

And although these past months have been extremely difficult, I am closer to God than I have ever been before. I used to focus on what was taken away from me. Now, I look back with thanksgiving in my heart. God allowed me to spend 18 amazing months with Brett before taking him to Heaven. James 4:14 says, "...You are a mist that appears for a little while and then vanishes.[37]" Some mists last longer than others. What matters is that we make the most of our mist.

I wasn't honoring God, or Brett, by harboring unforgiveness toward Blake. God saved both of us that night. We have work left to do. By the grace of God I have forgiven Blake and it has filled me with a peace that truly surpasses all human understanding. Whatever you are going through, whatever you have done or has been done to you, it is not beyond God. There is nothing that can separate us from Him. He is all you need, now and forever.

CHAPTER FORTY-FIVE

Mollie watched Blake as he read her words. Tears quietly streamed down his face. When he was done he gently placed the paper on the table and wiped his eyes.

"Mollie...it's, it's beautiful," he whispered.

"I started writing it yesterday. God placed it on my heart after I heard your testimony. God is changing lives through your testimony Blake. I know because it has changed me," she replied, unable to fight back her tears.

"God not only placed it on my heart to write this down," she continued. "I feel He has a plan for me and I need your help."

"My help?"

"I believe that God wants to use my story to reach others too. We both were saved from death that night. We both have work left to do on Earth and I think we are meant to do it...together."

Blake looked into Mollie's eyes, desperately searching to understand what she was implying.

"You see, when Ruby gives her testimony it is incredible. The same is true when James shares his. But, when they share together it is profound. People can relate with either or both of their stories. I think we can honor God, and Brett, by giving our testimonies...together."

"I would be honored."

After Mollie left, Blake went back to work but he couldn't stop thinking about her and their talk. When she said the word "together," Blake had secretly hoped that she meant more than just sharing their testimonies but that would be too much to ask for. *Lord, thank you for the opportunity to work with Mollie to reach others for You. You know my desire is to be with her, but if that is not Your will then please show me!*

W

Their first speaking engagement was only six days away so Mollie suggested meeting at the coffee shop near the shelter on Wednesday after Blake finished his shift. That was still two days away but Blake was already a nervous wreck. *Please Lord, give me the strength to do this. Please quiet my desires...*

That night, a renewed sense of purpose coursed through Mollie as she parked in front of Brooke and Derek's home. She was eager to tell Brooke about her meeting with Blake. But, instead, there was a note on the kitchen table.

Mollie,
I went to the grocery store. Will be back soon. A package arrived for you today. I put it on your bed.

Love,
Brooke

As Mollie reached for the package a smile crept across her face. Little did Brooke know that what lie inside that box was really for her. And the moment Brooke walked in the door with an armful of groceries she knew that Mollie was up to something.

"You sure seem to be in a good mood," Brooke chuckled.

"I am. Can you come with me into the living room?"

As soon as they sat down Mollie reached for two small boxes that were on the coffee table. She handed them to Brooke.

"What's this?" she asked.

"I guess you'll just have to open them and see," Mollie replied, her body trembling in anticipation.

Brooke carefully opened one of the boxes. She gasped and immediately began to sob.

"Oh Brooke! I'm so sorry!" Mollie exclaimed. "I didn't mean to make you..."

"No, Mollie. These are tears of joy. This is the most amazing gift I could have ever received! I will treasure this for as long as I live! Thank you," she said as she wrapped her arms around Mollie.

"I thought you could wear one and put the other one in the keepsake box your father made."

"Oh Mollie, it's absolutely perfect!" she whispered as she gently ran her finger over the pendant. On the front was Darlene's fingerprint and on the back it said, "Tenderly Loved Blessing."

Mollie was overwhelmed by Brooke's reaction. She gently touched the heart necklace that Brett made her. Suddenly, Mollie realized that she was still holding back, that she had not given all of herself to God and to His Great Commission. She knew what needed to be done.

W

Thankfully, the next two days were so hectic that Mollie's mind did not wander to thoughts of Blake and their meeting. It wasn't until she was driving to the coffee shop that she began thinking about him. Instantly, her stomach was tied into a million knots. *Please Lord help me! I don't know if I am nervous about speaking in front of strangers or of spending time with...him!*

Her body was trembling by the time she pulled into the parking lot. She took some deep breaths. *Lord, I need You!*

As soon as Mollie walked in she saw Blake. He was sitting at a table near the fireplace. She could tell that he was nervous too. They placed their orders and went back to the table.

"Yesterday I spoke with the pastor of the church we will be speaking at on Sunday. He is very excited that you will be joining me," Blake said, trying to break the ice.

"I wish I wasn't feeling so nervous about it. Speaking in front of strangers scares me to death," Mollie replied nervously.

"I am the same way. I was a nervous wreck the first time. It does seem to get a little easier each time. The pastor told me that this church has a more traditional sanctuary with pews, stained glass windows and a pulpit. Whenever I speak at churches like these I tend to look just above the heads of the congregation. As much as I would like to make eye contact, it seems to make me more nervous."

"Thanks! I think seeing all those eyes looking back at me would do me in," Mollie chuckled, trying to mask her anxiety.

By the time they were done with dinner they had gone over both of their testimonies and decided that Blake would speak first and Mollie would follow. She was amazed at how well they worked together. The only awkward moment was when they walked to their cars. Mollie could tell that Blake was unsure of what to say, or do, because she was feeling the same way.

"Would you like me to pick you up on Sunday or should we meet at the church?" he asked as they stopped in front of Mollie's car.

"Let's ride together."

"Wonderful! I'll pick you up at eight," he grinned.

"Perfect! See you then," Mollie replied as she got into her car.

W

Over the next few days, Mollie continued to work on the project God placed on her heart. She thought about telling Ruby or Brooke about it. Maybe even Blake. But, she decided to wait until she had everything in place. It was quickly becoming a much larger task than she first anticipated, but it would be worth it if it all came together.

Mollie barely slept Saturday night. She tossed and turned, imagining everything that could possibly go wrong. When she woke in the morning, she immediately reached for her Scripture journal and turned to the tab about worrying. "Do not be anxious about anything, but in every situation, by prayer and petition, with thanksgiving, present your requests to God.[41]"

Lord, thank You for this opportunity. I want to do Your will but I'm scared. Please help me. I can't do this without You!

She took deep breaths during the entire car ride with Blake. He seemed to understand and didn't try to make conversation. After meeting with the pastor and going over all the details, they were directed to an empty conference room to wait until it was time. Mollie paced the room the entire time. She couldn't sit still. *Breathe Mollie. Just breathe.* She could see the concern in Blake's eyes whenever she looked in his direction.

"Mollie, are you okay? I can do this alone if you're not…"

"It's okay. I'm okay. The waiting is the hardest part," she said breathlessly.

"Would it be okay if I…if I prayed for you?" he asked tentatively.

"Yes, please. I could use all the help I can get," Mollie said with a nervous laugh.

She assumed that Blake would bow his head and say a silent prayer for her. But, instead, he stood up and walked toward her. He placed his hands in hers and they instantly stopped shaking.

"Lord, please be with Mollie. May she feel Your peace and Your presence as she shares her testimony. My prayer for her is the same as Paul's prayer in Ephesians. Please give her the words to say and the confidence to say them fearlessly.[50] In Your name we pray, Amen."

They stood there for a moment, hand in hand. Mollie was speechless. What he did. What he said. She felt a calm come over her. Suddenly, the door opened and a young man told them that it was time to go.

"Thank you," Mollie whispered.

Blake just smiled and squeezed her hands.

As soon as they walked up to the front of the church, Mollie's anxiety returned. Seeing all the people made her stomach ache.

She sat down in the front pew as Blake walked up to the podium. Mollie tried to listen but her mind seemed to be spinning uncontrollably. With each passing minute, she felt herself getting more and more nervous. *Lord, please! Please help me!*

If it hadn't been for the applause, Mollie wouldn't have known that it was her turn to speak. She slowly stood up, her knees weak. She felt her whole body shaking as she walked up to the podium. Blake touched her arm and whispered, "You can do this. God is with you."

Mollie was thankful for the podium. It concealed her trembling from the congregation. However, as soon as she spoke, her cover was blown.

"Good morning. My name is Mollie Walker," she said, her voice wavering with each word. "Brett Walker was my husband," she cried. Mollie had been practicing all week but she still could not say those words without getting emotional. She took a few deep breaths and tried to compose herself. Suddenly, she felt someone gently place their hands on her shoulders.

Mollie felt a warmth come over her and her trembling subsided. There were still moments during her testimony when she became emotional but her anxiety had been replaced with an unexplainable peace.

The pastor invited them to stay after the service but Mollie was exhausted. They walked in silence to Blake's car. It wasn't until they were parked in front of Brooke and Derek's house that Blake spoke.

He looked at her, his eyes glistening. "Mollie, you were amazing."

"I don't think I could have done it if it weren't for you putting your hands on my shoulders," she replied as tears gathered in her eyes.

Blake's expression immediately changed and Mollie could tell that something wasn't right.

"Blake, what is it?"

"Mollie, I...I never left my seat. No one did."

"But I felt it. I know I did. It was just as real as when you held my hands," Mollie stammered.

Blake placed his hand on hers. "I believe you,"

When Mollie looked into Blake's eyes she could tell that he did. "Maybe it was God. Or maybe…" She couldn't finish. She didn't need to. Blake knew what she was thinking. "I…I have to go," she said   as   she   opened   the   car   door.

CHAPTER FORTY-SIX

Mollie was thankful that Derek and Brooke were not home. She needed some time to herself. Buster must have sensed that something was wrong and immediately followed Mollie to her room. He curled up next to her as she cried. *Lord, was that You? Was it...Brett?*

Some questions are not meant to be answered this side of Heaven. Yet, there was no doubt in Mollie's mind that someone had been with her that day. During the next few weeks, she would catch herself daydreaming about it; envisioning Jesus, or Brett, standing behind her, encouraging her, loving her. She began to wonder if it would happen again.

As difficult as it was for Mollie to tell her story, she noticed that her nervousness lessened each time she spoke. And each time, she waited with anticipation to feel those hands upon her, that peace to envelope her. But, she had not felt them since that first time.

It reminded her of the *Footprints in the Sand* poem by Mary Stevenson.[51] In the poem, the person sees that during the difficult times there is only one set of footprints and assumes that God was not there. God replies that those footprints are His, when He was carrying the believer. Mollie realized that God had been carrying her since she lost Brett. And now, she was ready for Him to walk beside her, to encourage and strengthen her. Feeling those hands placed upon her let her know that He is with her always, even if she can't feel Him.

And, Mollie wasn't the only one finding encouragement and strength. Brooke and Derek started going with Ruby and James to their support group. Mollie could already see the positive impact it was having on all of them. It reminded her of the verse Ruby shared from 2 Corinthians about how God comforts us in our struggles so that we can comfort others.[35] Mollie would quietly recite this verse every time before sharing her testimony, and it was this verse that prompted her to pursue her latest project and she couldn't wait to tell the others about it.

It was also that verse that finally gave Mollie the courage to agree to stay after the service to talk with members of the congregation. She and Blake had been giving their testimonies together for several weeks before she felt ready. Even after she agreed to it, she felt intimidated by the idea of speaking with people face to face.

Blake shared that he also had these same fears. But now, it is the part he looks forward to the most. The stories he has heard and the words of encouragement he has received from complete strangers has demonstrated the love of God to him in such profound ways.

Mollie soon realized that Blake was right. The people she has met, the stories she has heard, have touched her deeply. For her, it was her own little support group. It was living out the verse from 2 Corinthians.[35] So instead of dreading this time after their message, she looked forward to it with anticipation.

Mollie's mind began to recall their last speaking engagement. The service was over and she and Blake had just taken their places on either side of the front of the sanctuary. Mollie had closed her eyes for a moment and took a few deep breaths, preparing herself for whatever may come, when suddenly, someone threw their arms around her. In the shock of the moment Mollie almost lost her footing. At first, all Mollie could tell was that it was a woman who was hugging her. She waited as the woman cried in her arms. It wasn't until she stepped back that Mollie realized who it was.

"Mrs. Tate?" Mollie asked in disbelief.

"I am so sorry," she blurted. "I was so horrible to you. Can you ever forgive me?" she sobbed.

Mollie put her arms around her. "Of course I forgive you. I hope one day you can forgive me too," Mollie whispered.

"Oh Mollie, I have! I was so upset that day about Matthew being sent home that I completely forgot about what you have been through this year. By the time it all sank in I was too ashamed to apologize."

"All that matters is that we are here and we are forgiven," Mollie replied as she held her hands.

"Amen!" she exclaimed. "You know, I thought about not coming to church today but Matthew urged us to go. Now I know that God was speaking through him!"

As Blake and Mollie walked to his car, Mollie said a silent prayer, thanking God for orchestrating this moment to repair her relationship with Matthew's mother. She could tell that Blake was curious as to who the woman was but was afraid to ask. Mollie began telling him about the day she sent Matthew home by mistake and how angry his mother had been.

"I was devastated. She even wanted him moved to another classroom. When he didn't come to school right away the next day I thought she had removed him from the school altogether. But as soon as he arrived, I hugged him with all my might and told him how sorry I was. He forgave me with such ease, such love. I was overcome with a sense of peace because of his forgiveness. It was in that moment that I felt ready to meet you, to forgive you. But then..."

"Then you discovered that I was Steven," Blake added.

"I'm so sorry, Blake." Mollie placed her hand on his. "I...I think I was just overwhelmed. My mind was having a hard time wrapping itself around the fact that you and Steven were the same person." *It wasn't just my mind having a hard time...*

"I understand," he replied, squeezing her hand and trying to smile.

"What matters now is that we are here and we are forgiven," Mollie said, echoing the words she shared with Mrs. Tate.

"Exactly," he said as he looked deep into her eyes.

202

Mollie's nervousness about speaking may be subsiding but her nervousness around Blake...that was a whole different story. She could tell that she was blushing so she quickly changed the subject.

"There is something I have been working on and I would love your input," Mollie said.

"Of course. I can't wait to hear about it," Blake said as he parked in front of Brooke and Derek's house.

"They are probably still at church. Would you like to come in for lunch and I'll tell you all about it?"

"I'd love to."

Buster was overjoyed when he saw Blake walk in. They kept each other company while Mollie made lunch. As she told Blake about her idea his face lit up. He was thrilled about incorporating it into their message and was eager to help in any way he could.

W

After a few weeks of phone calls and meetings, Mollie and Blake were finally ready to launch their idea. They decided to invite their friends and family to their next speaking engagement and surprise them. They spoke with the pastor and arranged to have volunteers on hand to help after the service.

Mollie waited anxiously for her turn to speak. It was amazing that, even though she and Blake had given their testimonies numerous times, it had never diminished the emotions they felt as they spoke. Mollie assumed that her excitement for their announcement would distract her as she spoke but, instead, she was more emotional than ever before. Finally, she was at the conclusion of her speech. This was it.

"Shortly after the accident I found a gift bag in our closet and inside was the gift Brett intended to give me that night." Mollie clutched her necklace, desperately fighting back the tears.

"The gift was a necklace Brett had created just for me. It is a heart made from two hands. The chain goes through holes in the palms of the hands. They are the hands of Jesus. There had been a note with the necklace. In it, Brett spoke of John 15:13: There is no greater love than to lay down one's life for one's friends.[2] Little did Brett know that he would lay down his life for me. You see, when he saw Blake's car coming toward us he veered to the right which meant that the majority of the impact was on the driver's side, killing him immediately." Mollie took several deep breaths, trying to keep her composure.

"I have kept this necklace all to myself. When I wear it, it is like a part of Brett is still with me. Every time I look at it I think of him, and I think of Jesus. Brett sacrificed his life for me. Jesus laid down his life for all of us. I have realized that this necklace, and the message it gives, was intended for all, not just for me. Brett wanted to reach others for Christ. I believe that this necklace will fulfill his dream. If you would like one of Brett's *No Greater Love* necklaces they are available for purchase after the service in the church lobby.

"My prayer is that when this necklace hangs around your neck it will remind you of Jesus hanging on the cross, taking our sins upon Himself so that we may have eternal life with Him in Heaven. It is this hope, of spending eternity with Jesus and being reunited with loved ones, that brings me unexplainable peace and joy, no matter what may come in this life. And, it is this hope that drives us to share our stories and reach as many people for Christ as possible. There will be volunteers in the lobby to assist you and people on hand if you would like to talk with someone about having a personal relationship with Jesus. Thank you and God Bless," Mollie concluded, unsure how she was still managing to stand.

Immediately, the congregation stood and began clapping. As Mollie placed her hands on the podium to steady herself, she felt a hand on her shoulder. She turned to find Blake standing beside her. Even though she knew whose hand it was, she was still enveloped with the same warmth and peace as she felt that first time. As Mollie looked at him she saw that there were tears in his eyes as he smiled at the congregation. *Lord, is he here to walk beside me?*

W

The response to the necklace was so overwhelming that they had a website created to keep up with the demand. It was beyond anything Mollie could have imagined.

Between speaking engagements and managing the website, time seemed to fly by. Blake and Mollie were spending a lot of time together and she noticed that her feelings for him were deepening, but she still wasn't ready to tell him, to show him. And she could tell that Blake cared for her, especially in the way he looked at her. Mollie couldn't quite describe it, but there was something about him that reminded her of Brett.

W

Blake cherished every moment he got to spend with Mollie. The more he was with her, the deeper he was falling in love with her. He tried to fight it, to remind himself that it would be impossible for her to love him. But, no matter how hard he tried, or how fervently he prayed, he could not stop himself from loving her. Even though it may end up breaking his heart, Blake clung to the words Jesus said in Matthew, "With God all things are possible.[9]"

W

One Sunday, Mollie and Blake had just finished speaking together at a local church. After the service, they stood on either side of the stage ready to talk with anyone who had questions or stories of their own to share. A group of people had gathered around Blake. After talking with them he noticed a man walking up to him. Blake recognized him immediately.

"Judge Stevens?"

"Remember the last time we saw each other and I said that I hoped to never see your name again? Well, I was in my office the other day, thumbing through the paper, when I came upon an article written about you and these speaking engagements you have been doing. I remembered your case immediately.

"Over the years I have had victims' families write to me, asking for leniency on a sentencing or even hoping for an early release. When I received the letters on your behalf it was the one from the victim's sister that spoke to me in such a profound way. In her letter she said that she truly believes that everything happens for a reason, a reason ordained by God. And, as difficult as it has been for her to come to terms with the death of her brother, there must be a reason why God chose to spare your life and take his.

"She shared that, before his death, her brother planned to go to seminary to become a pastor. She has asked God over and over again why He would take someone so soon who planned to reach others in His name. The only answer she could surmise is that Brett would reach others for Christ *through you*. She was the one who suggested that, if you were granted early release, you would be required to tell your story at churches, organizations and such. She honestly believed that the more time you spent in prison, the less time you had to be out in the world impacting lives for Christ.

"Like I said in the courtroom, it was a combination of the letters and the report on overcrowding that resulted in your early release. But, honestly, it was her letter that played the greatest role in my decision. I prayed for God's wisdom and felt His nudge to proceed. I've been praying often that God would show me that I had made the right decision by letting you go. So, when I saw that you would be speaking here today I just had to come and hear it for myself. After listening to you and Mollie and seeing the love you share…"

Blake immediately interrupted, "Your Honor, we aren't…"

But the judge put up his hand to stop him. "Perhaps neither of you is ready to admit it yet but I know what I saw…what I see," he added. Blake saw Mollie approaching and instantly began blushing.

"And, it isn't the only thing I see with undeniable clarity. You see, I've always thought that if I tried to be a good person, was fair and honest in my work; that I would one day go to Heaven. But, after today I have realized that nothing I do will ever earn me a place in Heaven. It is only with a personal relationship with Jesus. So, thanks to you two, I've asked Jesus into my heart."

Tears began to gather in the corner of Blake's eyes and when he looked at Mollie tears were streaming down her cheeks. Blake put his hand out. Judge Stevens reached out and hugged him. It took Blake by surprise. They hugged for a long while and then Judge Stevens turned to Mollie and wrapped his arms around her. When he looked at Blake and Mollie they could see this light in his eyes. "God Bless you both and keep up the good work," he said with a smile and walked away.

"I have chills," Mollie whispered.

"Me too," Blake managed to say.

Mollie excused herself to use the restroom. She needed a moment alone. For several minutes she just stared into the mirror. She was amazed at the change that had taken place; not on the outside, but from within. And, the light in her eyes was all the proof she needed. She glanced down as she washed her hands. It was then that she realized that it was time...

Blake and Mollie sat in silence as Blake drove her home. They were both still in shock over seeing Judge Stevens and knowing that he had asked Jesus into his heart. Their hope has always been that, through their testimonies, they are reaching others for Christ. Today's events reaffirmed their mission.

As Blake parked in front of the house Mollie heard him gasp.

"Mollie! Your ring...you've lost your ring!" he shouted.

Mollie gently placed her hand on his. "It's not lost."

"But, you had it on this morning and now...now it's gone!" he said.

"I know. I took it off," she replied with a smile.

"Took it off? But why?" he asked.

"I have been wearing it to guard my heart until I am ready to..." she paused as tears welled up inside of her.

Blake's expression immediately softened and he placed his hand on top of hers.

"However long it takes. I'll wait forever if I have to," he whispered, his eyes glistening.

Mollie looked deep into Blake's eyes as tears gathered in hers and whispered, "I have a feeling you won't have to wait that long."

W

Want to read an excerpt from the next book in the series:
Worth Working For
and be the first to know when it is available?

Want your very own *No Greater Love Necklace*?
Please visit my website:

www.angiebathobarth.com

References

1. "I know the plans that I have for you, declares the Lord, plans for prosperity and not for calamity, to give you a future and a hope" (based on Jeremiah 29:11). www.christianbook.com CBD Christian Gifts Item RF96269Y.

2. "There is no greater love than to lay down one's life for one's friends" (John 15:13 New Living Translation). Bible Gateway. Web. 15 Feb. 2015.

3. "Trust in the LORD with all your heart and lean not on your own understanding" (Proverbs 3:5 New International Version). Bible Gateway. Web. 15 Feb. 2015.

4. "Thy word is a lamp unto my feet, and a light unto my path" (Psalm 119:105 King James Version). Bible Gateway. Web. 15 Feb. 2015.

5. "May the peace of God, which surpasses all understanding, guard your heart and your mind in Christ Jesus" (based on Phil. 4:7). *A Pocket Guide to Prayer.* Steve Harper. Upper Room Books, 2012. Print.

6. "And do not neglect doing good and sharing; for with such sacrifices God is pleased" (Hebrews 13:16 New American Standard Bible). Bible Hub. Web. 15 Feb. 2015.

7. "If any of you lacks wisdom, you should ask God, who gives generously to all without finding fault, and it will be given to you" (James 1:5 New International Version). Bible Hub. Web. 15 Feb. 2015.

8. "Count it all joy, my brothers, when you meet trials of various kinds, for you know that the testing of your faith produces steadfastness. And let steadfastness have its full effect, that you may be perfect and complete, lacking in nothing" (James 1:2-4 English Standard Version). Bible Hub. Web 18 Feb. 2015.

9. "Jesus looked at them and said, "With man this is impossible, but with God all things are possible" (Matt. 19:26 New International Version). Bible Gateway. Web. 15 Feb. 2015.

10. "...be quick to listen, slow to speak and slow to become angry" (James 1:19 New International Version). Bible Hub. Web. 18 Feb. 2015.

11. "Consider it pure joy, my brothers and sisters, whenever you face trials of many kinds, because you know that the testing of your faith produces perseverance" (James 1:2-3 New International Version). Bible Hub. Web. 18 Feb. 2015.

12. "...For the mouth speaks what the heart is full of" (Matthew 12:34 New International Version). Bible Hub. Web 18 Feb. 2015.

13. "but no human being can tame the tongue. It is a restless evil, full of deadly poison" James 3:8 New International Version). Bible Hub. Web. 18 Feb. 2015.

14. "The tongue has the power of life and death..." (Proverbs 18:21 New International Version). Bible Hub. Web 18 Feb. 2015.

15. "The thief comes only to steal and kill and destroy; I have come that they may have life, and have it to the full" (John 10:10 New International Version). Bible Hub. Web. 18 Feb. 2015.

16. Rau, Andy. (2012, July 25) Why Does God Allow Tragedy and Suffering? Retrieved from https://www.biblegateway.com/blog/2012/07/why-does-god-allow-tragedy-and-suffering/

17. "And we know that in all things God works for the good of those who love Him, who have been called according to His purpose" (Romans 8:28 New International Version). Bible Hub. Web 18 Feb. 2015.

18. "For I consider that the sufferings of this present time are not worth comparing with the glory that is to be revealed to us" (Romans 8:18 English Standard Version). Bible Hub. Web. 18 Feb. 2015.

19. Hall, M., West M. and Herms, B. (2012). Already There [Recorded by Casting Crowns]. *Come to the Well* [CD]. Franklin, TN: Zoo Studio.

20. "Religion that God our Father accepts as pure and faultless is this: to look after orphans and widows in their distress and to keep oneself from being polluted by the world" (James 1:27 New International Version). Bible Hub. Web. 21 Feb. 2015.

21. Guder Triplett, E. & Hoherd, M. (2012) James Lessons 1-6. Colorado Springs, CO: Community Bible Study.

22. "There is only one Lawgiver and Judge, the one who is able to save and destroy. But you--who are you to judge your neighbor?" (James 4:12 New International Version). Bible Hub. Web. 21 Feb. 2015.

23. Ruymann, A. (2012) James Lessons 1-6. Colorado Springs, CO: Community Bible Study.

24. West, M. (2012). Forgiveness [Recorded by Matthew West]. *Into the Light* [CD]. Brentwood, TN: Sparrow.

25. "For I know the plans I have for you," declares the LORD, "plans to prosper you and not to harm you, plans to give you hope and a future" (Jeremiah 29:11 New International Version). Bible Hub. Web. 21 Feb. 2015.

26. "But he gives more grace. Therefore it says, "God opposes the proud, but gives grace to the humble" (James 4:6 English Standard Version). Bible Hub. Web. 21 Feb. 2015.

27. Ingram, J., Donehey, M. and Owen, J. (2012). Worn [Recorded by Tenth Avenue North]. *The Struggle* [CD]. Brentwood, TN: Reunion.

28. Donehey, M., Ingram, J. and LaRue, P. (2008). By Your Side [Recorded by Tenth Avenue North]. *Over and Underneath* [CD]. Brentwood, TN: Reunion.

29. "Behold, I stand at the door and knock. If anyone hears my voice and opens the door, I will come in to him and eat with him, and he with me" (Revelations 3:20 English Standard Version). Bible Hub. Web. 22 Feb. 2015.

30. "If you confess with your mouth that Jesus is Lord and believe in your heart that God raised him from the dead, you will be saved" (Romans 10:9 New Living Translation). Bible Hub. Web. 22 Feb. 2015.

31. Unknown. (2015). The Sinner's Prayer. *Into the Light Ministries.*
Retrieved from http://www.intothelight.org/answers/sinners-
prayer.asp.

32. Garcia, D.A., Glover, B., Reyes, B. and Reyes, J. (2012. He Said
[Recorded by Group 1 Crew feat. Chris August]. *Fearless* [CD].
Nashville, TN: Fervent/Curb/Word.

33. Muckala, D., Ingram, J., Fuqua, M., Havens, J. and Muckala, D.
(2010.) Light Up the Sky [Recorded by The Afters]. *Light Up the Sky*
[CD]. Brentwood, TN: INO.

34. Stevens, C., Glover, B. and Garcia, D. (2013). Overcomer
[Recorded by Mandisa]. *Overcomer* [CD]. Brentwood, TN: Sparrow.

35. "He comforts us in all our troubles so that we can comfort
others..." (2 Corinthians 1:4 New Living Translation). Bible Hub.
Web. 8 March 2015.

36. "Instead, you ought to say, 'If it is the Lord's will, we will live and
do this or that'" (James 4:15 New International Version). Bible Hub.
Web. 26 Feb. 2015.

37. "Why, you do not even know what will happen tomorrow.
What is your life? You are a mist that appears for a little while and
then vanishes" (James 4:14 New International Version). Bible Hub.
Web. 8 March 2015.

38. "...Well done, good and faithful servant..." (Matthew 25:23 New
International Version). Bible Hub. Web. 8 March 2015

39. Alexander, E. (2010). *The Summit.* Green Forest, AR: New Leaf Press.

40. "So do not fear, for I am with you; do not be dismayed, for I am your God. I will strengthen you and help you; I will uphold you with my righteous right hand" (Isaiah 41:10 New International Version). Bible Hub. Web. 7 March 2015.

41. "Do not be anxious about anything, but in every situation, by prayer and petition, with thanksgiving, present your requests to God. And the peace of God, which transcends all understanding, will guard your hearts and your minds in Christ Jesus" (Philippians 4:6-7 New International Version). Bible Hub. Web. 7 March 2015.

42. "Cast all your anxiety on him because he cares for you" (1 Peter 5:7 New International Version). Bible Hub. Web. 7 March 2015.

43. "Peace I leave with you; My peace I give to you. Not as the world gives do I give to you. Let not your hearts be troubled, neither let them be afraid" (John 14:27 English Standard Version). Bible Hub. Web. 7 March 2015.

44. "When I am afraid, I put my trust in you" (Psalm 56:3 English Standard Version). Bible Hub. Web. 7 March 2015.

45. "Even though I walk through the valley of the shadow of death, I will fear no evil, for you are with me; your rod and your staff, they comfort me" (Psalm 23:4 English Standard Version). Bible Hub. Web. 7 March 2015.

46. "Put on the full armor of God, so that you can take your stand against the devil's schemes" (Ephesians 6:11 New International Version). Bible Hub. Web 8 March 2015.

47. "For to me, living means living for Christ, and dying is even better" (Philippians 1:21 New Living Translation). Bible Hub. Web. 8 March 2015

48. "But if I live, I can do more fruitful work for Christ" (Philippians 1:22 New Living Translation). Bible Hub. Web. 8 March 2015.

49. "Stay alert! Watch out for your great enemy, the devil. He prowls around like a roaring lion, looking for someone to devour" (1 Peter 5:8 New Living Translation). Bible Hub. Web. 8 March 2015.

50. "Pray also for me, that whenever I speak, words may be given me so that I will fearlessly make known the mystery of the gospel, for which I am an ambassador in chains. Pray that I may declare it fearlessly, as I should" (Ephesians 6:19-20 New International Version). Bible Hub. Web. 8 March 2015.

51. Stevenson, Mary (1936). Footprints in the Sand. *Footprints in the Sand.* Retrieved on 08 March 2015 from http://www.footprints-inthe-sand.com/index.php?page=Poem/Poem.php.

CPSIA information can be obtained
at www.ICGtesting.com
Printed in the USA
LVOW10s0143100118

562500LV00009BA/303/P